THE CRUX

DUKE
UNIVERSITY
PRESS

DURHAM
AND LONDON
2003

Charlotte Perkins Gilman

THE CRUX

INTRODUCTION BY DANA SEITLER

"The Crux" was originally
published by Charlotte
Perkins Gilman in 1911.
Printed in the United
States of America on
acid-free paper ∞
Designed by R. Giménez
Typeset in Monotype
Bulmer by Keystone
Typesetting, Inc.
Library of Congress
Cataloging-in-Publication
Data appear on the last
printed page of this book.

CONTENTS

ACKNOWLEDGMENTS

I am grateful to Cathy N. Davidson and Priscilla Wald, who both encouraged me to pursue my interests in *The Crux* and provided me with helpful tips on how to do so. I am also indebted to Ken Wissoker for his support and editorial guidance, and to the anonymous readers of Duke University Press for their insightful suggestions for contextualizing *The Crux* in various American political, cultural, and literary histories. For more than savvy readings of multiple drafts of this introduction and for thoughtful and thought provoking discussions about the subject, I thank Cannon Schmitt.

INTRODUCTION

Like many other women writers of her day, including Kate Chopin, Sarah Orne Jewett, and Willa Cather, Charlotte Perkins Gilman used her prose to facilitate social change for women and to enter into the growing fray of sexual politics—usually by presenting her readers with guidance and instruction through exemplary characters. In her original preface to *The Crux* (1911), she states: "This story is, first, for young women to read; second, for young men to read; after that, for anybody who wants to." Gilman wrote elsewhere that she hoped to create a genre that would reflect "the new attitude of the full grown woman, who faces the demands of love with the highest standards of conscious motherhood."[1] In fact, she considered her body of work as a remedy for the "ills of modernity," what she characterizes in *Women and Economics* (1898) as a time in which "human motherhood is more pathological than any other, more morbid, defective, irregular, diseased."[2] It should come as no surprise that *The Crux* is filled with the trappings of these desires, leading some scholars to criticize her body of work as didactic, or, as biographer Ann Lane puts it, "as lessons."[3] In her autobiography, Gilman reflected on the challenge fiction writing posed for her: "The stories . . . called for composition

1. Charlotte Perkins Gilman, *Man-Made World, Our Androcentric Culture* (New York: Charlton, 1911), 179.
2. Charlotte Perkins Gilman, *Women and Economics* (1898; reprint, New York: Prometheus Books, 1996), 181.
3. Ann Lane, ed. *The Charlotte Perkins Gilman Reader* (New York: Pantheon Books, 1980), xvi.

and were more difficult–especially the novels, which are poor."[4] In the case of *The Crux,* we might be tempted to agree: the novel is more of a political accomplishment than an aesthetic one. However, as I discuss later, *The Crux,* set within its historical and cultural context, not only sheds light on Gilman's social and political concerns, but also, ungainly as her plot devices may sometimes be, experiments rather radically with the generic conventions of the era.

First, however, it is important to understand the larger context within which the recent republication of Gilman's texts has taken place. In 1973 the Feminist Press reprinted "The Yellow Wallpaper" (1892), with an afterword by Gilman scholar Elaine Hedges. In the 1970s Hedges played a crucial role in helping to revive Gilman and other women writers of the nineteenth century, bringing "The Yellow Wallpaper" to national attention. Earlier, in 1966, Carl Degler reissued *Women and Economics,* which also encouraged Gilman scholarship. Mary Hill's well-known biography appeared in 1980, after which, in 1985, Gary Scharnhorst wrote a comprehensive and useful bibliography of primary and secondary sources. In 1989, Sheryl L. Meyering put out one of the first collections of critical essays on Gilman, a major effort in the feminist critical engagement with her more well-known texts.[5] Unfortunately, though, Gilman's extraordinary record of publication has been only selectively recovered for scholarly and political use. In addition to her more well-known work, such as "The Yellow Wallpaper" and the socialist-feminist treatise *Women and Economics,* Gilman was the author of many other works of fiction and nonfiction that contributed to the shape and structure of American politics. Yet while her better-known works have been granted a particular salience in contemporary feminist criticism, her lesser-known materials have been largely marginalized.

Thus, despite the effort of recovery, *The Crux* has received little

4. Charlotte Perkins Gilman, *The Living of Charlotte Perkins Gilman: An Autobiography* (1935; reprint, New York: Arno Press, 1972), 100.

5. Gilman's popularity with feminist literary critics continued when, in 1990, in collaboration with Shelly Fishkin, Hedges founded the Charlotte Perkins Gilman Society. The formation of the society inspired several conferences focusing exclusively on Gilman's work, including the First International Charlotte Perkins Gilman Conference, held in Liverpool in 1995, and the Second International Conference, held in New York at Skidmore College in 1997.

attention or recognition since its initial publication in 1911. It first appeared serially in Gilman's own magazine, *The Forerunner,* in 1910; it was then published separately a year later by her publishing group the Charlton Company. Since then, *The Crux* has been reissued in a reader in 1980, in which editor Ann Lane excerpted three of the novel's 311 pages. Lane's reader and other efforts by the feminist press and feminist literary critics mark the beginning of a movement to reclaim and recover Gilman's more obscure texts. This publication of the full text of *The Crux* will, I hope, be central to how we continue to understand Gilman's body of work specifically and the complicated literary landscape of early feminism more generally.

In many ways, *The Crux* presents us with a familiar Gilman: its didacticism, female-centered narrative, and socialist critique of patriarchal power relations all correspond to twentieth-century critics' gender-based narrative readings of texts such as "The Yellow Wallpaper" and *Herland* (1914). But *The Crux* also complicates this critical history because, for one thing, it more fully illustrates the biological argument undergirding Gilman's feminism. For another, it demonstrates how Gilman played with generic conventions as a means to grapple with ideological ones. The novel tells the story of an intergenerational set of white female New England friends and relatives who relocate to Colorado to start a boarding house for men. At its most basic, the plot relates how the central character, the innocent Vivian Lane, falls for Morton Elder, who has both gonorrhea and syphilis. The concern of the novel, however, is not so much whether Vivian will catch syphilis, but that she may decide to marry and have children with the syphilitic Morton, thus weakening the "national stock." The antidote to Vivian's problems comes in the form of eugenic science so that, as Vivian's grandmother tells her, "We can religiously rid the world of all these—'undesirable citizens.'"

Despite the novel's eugenic leanings, typical characterizations of Gilman's work do not account for the ways in which her feminism was inextricable from her eugenic thinking. In fact, to date virtually no criticism exists on *The Crux.* Perhaps this is due to its lack of availability, perhaps also to the reluctance of feminist critics to disparage one of our literary foremothers. But to ignore this text is to ignore how it addresses, clearly and remarkably, the insecurities over contagion and disease that were rampant at the fin de siècle. *The*

Crux can be read as an allegory of the changing political and social anxieties of the early twentieth century. When Vivian Lane learns that "there is no forgiveness" for "biological sin," she is not only transported from the sheltered knowledge of adolescence to the dangers of adult modern love, she is placed within a scientific narrative about reproductive responsibility. Indeed, *The Crux* demonstrates how popular conceptions of eugenic science were attractive to feminist authors and intellectuals because they offered them the means to redefine their relationships to both reproduction and gender. As Louise Newman argues in *White Women's Rights,* evolutionary and eugenic constructions of racial progress and sexual difference were central to the ways in which white women activists in the late nineteenth and twentieth centuries conceptualized issues of equality, making it possible "for white women to overlook the ways in which white culture was implicated in systems of oppression that governed the lives of nonwhite women."[6] *The Crux* allows readers and teachers of Gilman to take a closer look at how issues of eugenics, reproduction, sexual disease, and motherhood helped shape and were shaped by her work, and it allows us to see the connection between feminist literary production and reproductive ideologies at the fin de siècle.[7]

As many scholars have pointed out, one way to understand the source of Gilman's philosophies is through the biographical details of her life. For instance, Ann Lane links her work to the primary relationships in her life—positive and negative—with her mother, father, female friends, daughter, two husbands, and therapist, calling Gilman's self-portraits "emotionally true."[8] Similarly, Mary Hill creates a kind of bildungsroman out of Gilman's life, producing a narrative of her individual development and perseverance that culminates in triumphant knowledge and self-realization. In so doing, she divides Gilman into "two opposing natures . . . the public image, rational and cool [and] the private self, compelling in its emotional

6. Louise Newman, *White Women's Rights: The Racial Origins of Feminism in the United States* (New York: Oxford University Press, 1999), 8.

7. For a more detailed analysis of the text see my article "Unnatural Selection: Mothers, Eugenic Feminism, and Charlotte Perkins Gilman's Regeneration Narratives," *American Quarterly* 55:5 (March 2003).

8. Ann Lane, *To Herland and Beyond: The Life and Work of Charlotte Perkins Gilman* (New York: Pantheon, 1990), xiii.

complexity."[9] For Hill, Gilman's feminist convictions and reformist drive rested in this duality.

While the biographical approach can yield significant information about an author's choices, it doesn't come without problems. Not only can it allow for too easy a bracketing of the mediated relationships between text and context in a novel and reduce some of the more dynamic properties of narrative form, but biography can also at times drift into hagiography due to the presentist intentions of the biographer in question. Therefore, my own version of Gilman's biography is a selective account of her life in relation to her work, but one that will, at least partially, serve to illuminate and clarify the influence of her personal and social context on her own thinking. In particular, I highlight those moments in Gilman's life that most clearly seem to have lent *The Crux* its particular shape and substance.

Born in 1860 in Hartford, Connecticut, Charlotte Perkins was the child of Mary Westcott Perkins and Frederick Beecher Perkins, of the New England Beecher family (Harriet Beecher Stowe was Gilman's great aunt). Her father abandoned the family when she was still a young child, leaving her mother, who finally divorced her father in 1873, to raise Charlotte and her brother Thomas alone. In 1878 Gilman briefly attended the Rhode Island School of Design. In 1883 she became a governess and in 1884 married her first husband, Charles Walter Stetson. Katherine Beecher Stetson, their only child, was born a year later—after which Gilman famously suffered from postpartum depression, an experience she would later write about in "The Yellow Wallpaper." As an antidote to her depression, Gilman underwent therapy with Silas Weir Mitchell and experienced his famous "rest cure" first hand. The rest cure called for little or no activity. For Gilman, Mitchell specifically prescribed that she discontinue all writing activities, as he felt these were causing her stress and anxiety. The rest cure not only failed to help Gilman, it inflamed her depressed state, inducing feelings of suicide. Explaining the effects of the cure, Gilman wrote: "I went home, followed those directions rigidly for months, and came perilously close to losing my mind."[10]

9. Mary Hill, *The Making of a Radical Feminist* (Philadelphia: Temple University Press, 1980), 44, 9.
10. Gilman, *Living*, 96.

Ultimately, following popular characterizations of the West as a curative region, she decided to winter in Pasadena, California as a way to improve her health.[11] Her stay in Pasadena would greatly influence her fiction in short stories such as "Bee Wise," in which a group of women settle in California to create a Fordist economic community, and in *The Crux,* where the women travel west to find themselves and their independence.

In 1888 Gilman decided to separate from Stetson. She took her daughter Kate to Pasadena to live with her close friend Grace Ellery Channing, whom she credits in her autobiography with "sav[ing] what there is of me."[12] In 1894 Stetson and Gilman divorced, and Gilman continued to collaborate with her friend Grace on writing and acting in drawing-room comedies. Grace and Stetson eventually married, and together they raised Gilman's daughter Kate with Gilman's consent. Her approval of this arrangement prompted many public disparagements of her own moral character.

In 1891 she met Adeline Knapp, with whom "she sincerely hoped to live continually" and for whom she felt "really passionate love."[13] Gilman's intimate friendship with Knapp, both figuratively sensual and platonic, played an essential role in her life and her writing, in which she repeatedly details the strength same-sex friendships afforded her female characters.[14] In 1894 she moved to San Francisco, where she edited *The Impress,* a publication of the Pacific Coast Women's Press Association. For the next several years Gilman continued her feminist activities, touring the country giving lectures at the Suffrage Association Convention in Washington, D.C., Hull House, and the International Socialist and Labor Union Congress in

11. See Jennifer S. Tuttle, "Rewriting the West Cure: Charlotte Perkins Gilman, Owen Wister, and the Sexual Politics of Neuresthenia," in *The Mixed Legacy of Charlotte Perkins Gilman,* eds. Catherine Golden & Joanna Schneider Zangrando (Newark: University of Delaware Press, 2000).

12. Hill, 161.

13. Quoted in Carol Farley Kessler, *Charlotte Perkins Gilman: Her Progress toward Utopia with Selected Writings* (New York: Syracuse University Press, 1995), 25.

14. On the prevalence of such same-sex friendships that were not necessarily "lesbian" as we understand and define the term today see Carroll Smith-Rosenberg, "The Female World of Love and Ritual: Relations Between Women in Nineteenth-Century America," in *Disorderly Conduct: Visions of Gender in Victorian America* (New York: Oxford University Press, 1985).

London, among other places. In 1900 she married again, this time to George Houghton Gilman (a relationship documented in her letters to him in Mary A. Hill's *A Journey from Within*). Gilman died in 1935 of suicide by chloroform after having been diagnosed with breast cancer.

Throughout her life Gilman was an avid reader of a variety of texts, including the fiction of Edward Bellamy, Elizabeth Stuart Phelps, and William Dean Howells, as well as the scientific treatises of Herbert Spencer, Lester Ward, and Patrick Geddes (especially his 1889 tract *The Evolution of Sex*). Following Bellamy's philosophy articulated in his utopian novel *Looking Backward,* which advanced a theory of evolutionary change through cooperation and community as opposed to Social Darwinian competition or Marxian revolution, Gilman became a "Nationalist." In 1896 she met one of her scientific mentors, Lester Ward, a paleobotanist turned sociologist who espoused a theory of "gynaecocracy," or the superiority of the female sex type. In 1900 she entered into her most prolific period of writing. Over the next twenty-one years, she published twelve books of verse, fiction, and nonfiction, while single-handedly editing *The Forerunner,* a serial that would eventually run to nine volumes. In 1909 she formed her own publishing house, the Charlton Company. *The Forerunner,* where *The Crux* first appeared, was distributed in the United States and abroad by the National American Suffrage Association, the Women's Political Union, and the Socialist Literature Company. Additional paid subscriptions totaled 1,500 per year at $1.00 per subscription.

While this is but a thumbnail sketch of Gilman's life and travels, it does begin to suggest the way her feminist practices and literary production transect tricky issues about reproduction, gender, domesticity, and nationalism in ways that make *The Crux* an ideal addition to the ongoing dialogue on race, American expansionism, social space, utopian fiction, sexuality, citizenship, and the public sphere.

Those with particular interests in issues of domesticity and its reformulation by women writers in the twentieth century will find Gilman a useful and complicated source. Polly Wynn Allen approaches Gilman's work by considering the relationship between feminism and spatial geographies in her fiction, developing in texts like *Herland* "non-sexist landscapes" and "the unified construction of neighborhoods" in which women, as mothers and laborers, reside.[15] Similarly, *The Crux* concerns women establishing living arrangements outside of a recognizably patriarchal model (a boardinghouse run by women) and can be seen in direct relationship to Gilman's other work on the socialized home in such texts as *What Diantha Did* (1910), in which a female heroine revolutionizes the housework and hotel industry in California, *Women and Economics,* and *The Home: Its Work and Influence* (1903). Her theories of domestic efficiency sponsored the "kitchenless home" and socialized child-care.[16] Gilman argued that the conventions of housewifery were part of a sexuo-economic contract obliging a woman to "get her living by getting a husband," or, more crassly, by exchanging sex for sustenance.[17] To disrupt the regulatory connection between sex and domestic survival, Gilman advocated that women obtain careers and establish communal eating arrangements for their families instead of providing for the cooking themselves. In this sense, the boardinghouse setting for *The Crux* is both a typical and an atypical domestic arrangement—the boardinghouse is a "business" owned and operated by women, but they establish it as a means to care for the men working the silver mines in Colorado: "the place was filled with men who needed mothering." In other words, it rests on the principle (for Gilman a scientific one) that as mothers women were responsible for the care and regeneration of not only men, but of "the race" as a whole.

Other critics, like Minna Doskow, position Gilman within the tradition of utopian writing: "By bringing women from the margins into the center, Gilman opened a new chapter in the utopian literary corpus."[18] Similarly, following Jane Tompkins's suggestion that the

15. Polly Wynn Allen, *Building Domestic Liberty: Charlotte Perkins Gilman's Architectural Feminism* (Amherst: University of Massachusetts Press, 1988), 175.

16. See Charlotte Perkins Gilman, "Kitchen-Mindedness," *Forerunner* 1 (Feb. 1910): 7–11; "The New Motherhood" *Forerunner* 1 (Dec. 1910): 17–18; and *The Home: Its Work and Influence* (New York: McClure, Philips & Co., 1903).

17. Gilman, *Women and Economics,* 110.

18. Minna Doskow, *Charlotte Perkins Gilman's Utopian Novels: Moving the Mountain, Herland, and With Her in Ourland* (Teaneck: Farleigh Dickinson University Press, 1999), 27.

“cultural work” of literary texts “attempt[s] to redefine the social order,” Carol Kessler is interested in “how Gilman developed her capacity to imagine utopia” in order to “affect reader’s lives substantially.”[19] Readers of Gilman may be more familiar with her utopian novels *Moving the Mountain* (published the same year as *The Crux,* 1911) and *Herland.* In each, the female inhabitants of Gilman’s utopias transform and at times entirely remake the world around them (as in *Herland,* whose inhabitants reproduce parthenogenetically—without the need of men or heterosexual intercourse). In both novels, we can read a longing to create compensatory feminist utopias as a means to solve the perceived problems of modernity. As I suggested earlier, these “fictions of progress,” for Gilman, seemed to secure white women’s centrality to cultural evolution, allowing them to experience reproduction as a world-making practice.

In *The Crux,* many of these utopian elements are present, especially in the treatment of the West as a natural and regenerative space to which the women travel so that they may forge a more progressive community. The new liberating community is, in many ways, predictable in that it acts as a blueprint for future change. But unlike other utopian novels, *The Crux* takes place in real time and relies upon actually existing social resources. In fact, *The Crux* revises our understanding of Gilman’s other novels. *The Crux* exemplifies a culture in uneasy transition, eschewing the vestiges of New England Puritanism for what is represented as the enlightened sexual-civic discourse of the West. It is an important piece of work, for it complicates what we know about the feminist and eugenicist writings of the period and allows us to view Gilman’s body of work in a new fashion. Positioned between the 1898 publication of “The Yellow Wallpaper” and the 1915 publication of *Herland, The Crux* asks that we reread these more studied works differently, and points specifically to the development of the eugenic/regenerative rhetoric dramatized within them.

The Crux, in this sense, is what I would call a “regeneration narrative,” which both inhabits and unsettles the “male” genres in-

19. Jane Tompkins, *Sensational Designs: The Cultural Work of American Fiction 1790–1860* (New York: Oxford University Press, 1985), xi; Kessler, *Charlotte Perkins Gilman: Her Progress toward Utopia,* 1–2.

tent on producing masculinity as an index for national regeneration. Western and adventure novels such as those made popular by Zane Grey and Owen Wister respond to Teddy Roosevelt's call for men to "gird up our loins as a nation, with stern purpose to play our part manfully in winning the ultimate triumph."[20] Richard Slotkin has characterized the typically male genres of the western and the adventure novel as performing a "regeneration through violence" in which the articulation of masculine strength through martial rhetoric guarantees American national superiority over its dominated others. *The Crux*—like the regeneration scenario that Slotkin describes—in part depends upon the narrative logic of the western or adventure novel that prescribes a separation from modern life and a temporary regression to a more "natural" state. Yet by simultaneously foregrounding the economic autonomy of women and their reproductive status, *The Crux* suggests that ideologies of national progress (including U.S. expansionism and the project of empire) have depended upon the energies of motherhood at least as much as those of masculine contest. The men in the novel moved to Colorado to try to win their fortunes in the silver mines, a plot that rehearses the conventions of the male western. However, the women's westward movement reconfigures the symbolic logic of a more traditional western plot, especially a novel like Owen Wister's *The Virginian,* where a New England greenhorn travels west in order to realize his own sense of "manliness." In *The Crux,* the women move west both to rejuvenate themselves and to forge a "home"—a space of gendered care—within its open spaces.[21]

The Crux thus means to derail the ideals of masculinity that the western and adventure genres tend to establish by replacing typically male protagonists with a series of college-educated, white, middle-

20. Theodore Roosevelt, "National Duties," in *The Strenuous Life: Essays and Addresses* (1910; reprint, St. Clair Shores, Michigan: Scholarly Press, 1970), 280.

21. An interesting addendum to this comparison is that Owen Wister was diagnosed with neurasthenia by the physician S. W. Mitchell (infamous for his "rest cure"). But unlike Gilman, Wister was not advised to "rest," but, rather, to take a trip out West for some exercise. In fact, while Gilman wrote "The Yellow Wallpaper" as a critique of Mitchell's therapy, Wister wrote *The Virginian* in praise of it. See Barbara Will, "The Nervous Origins of the American Western," *American Literature,* 70:2 (June 1998): 293–316.

class women. As in the western, in Gilman's fiction many of the female characters "go west" to find themselves and regain their health, their sanity, and their bodies in the open spaces where they engage in rigorous outdoor activity, as opposed to "rest." The transformation of these masculine genres seems to be a way for Gilman to reimagine her own and other women's social status. In this way, these "Westward expansions" act as an analog for the expansion of feminine identity. But perhaps more curiously, this new identity acts as an analog for evolutionary progress: Gilman's women do not only go west, but they also go "up." She often describes her female characters as dwelling in "upland valleys" surrounded by "steep canyons," and "the clean, wide, brilliant stillness of the high plateau," or even residing in sanatoriums called "The Hills" where they experience "the delight of mere ascent."[22] Geographical elevation is highlighted in Gilman's fiction not only as a representative aspiration in narratives which are insistently conscious of women's domestic confinement, but also as a Darwinian allegory of evolution where one's physical ascent to a higher place guarantees the commensurate logics of superior social status, economic mobility, health, and moral being.[23]

An enthusiastic reader of theories of civilization, evolution, and degeneration, Gilman's work refunctions the Darwinian concept of "natural selection" into a theory of social evolution prescribed, in part, by Herbert Spencer, to whom she referred in her autobiography

22. These quotes are from Gilman's different fictions: namely "Beewise," in *The Yellow Wallpaper and Other Stories* (New York: Oxford University Press, 1995), 226; *The Crux;* and "Dr. Clair's Place," in *The Yellow Wallpaper and Other Stories* (New York: Oxford University Press, 1995), 297.

23. Susan Lanser points out the racial politics of Gilman's work, noting how, even in her utopic novels, Gilman equates class and racial status with preparedness for socialist living, repeatedly claiming to favor immigration as long as immigrants are of better "stock." For instance, in *With Her in Ourland,* the sequel to *Herland,* the main character Ellador claims that you cannot "put a little of everything in the melting pot and produce a good metal," especially if those metals are "gold, silver, copper and iron, lead, radium, pipe, clay, and plain dirt." Charlotte Perkins Gilman, *With Her in Ourland* (1916; reprinted in *Charlotte Perkins Gilman's Utopian Novels,* ed. Minna Doskow (Madison and Teaneck: Farleigh University Press, London: Associated University Presses, 1999), 323.

as the man who taught her "wisdom and how to apply it."[24] Spencer asserted that evolution created qualitative and quantitative differences between male and female physiologies, and that when the body and brain were challenged energy set aside for reproduction would be used up. In other words, if cerebral activity in women was excessive, there would be losses in energy needed for "race-maintenance."[25] For Spencer, the body was a closed and finite system, one that required a balance between the physical or mental depletion in one area and the preservation of energy in a different one, a process he identified as the body's need for "equilibrium."[26] According to Spencer, the body's system of economization and expenditure of its mental and physical resources was differentiated and regulated by a gendered physiological economy: a greater portion of women's energy should be designated for reproductive activities, leaving them with less strength for other forms of labor or intellectual pursuit. Of course, Gilman found his antifeminist characterization of women disturbing. But in the theories of Lester Frank Ward, she found a way to reinterpret Spencer's blind spots when it came to women's physiological nature. Relying on Ward's emphasis on the female sex as the primary factor of hereditary transmission, Gilman argued that while both sexes were vulnerable to the conditions of modern life and labor, it was the female sex who, "as the race type," held the most immediate opportunity "through the immeasurable power of social motherhood" to "develop a race far more intelligent, efficient, and well-organized, living naturally at a much higher level of social progress."[27] (It should come as no surprise that, at the start of *The Crux,* Gilman describes Vivian as enthusiastically reading Lester Ward's theories.) Following Ward, socially responsible motherhood required an evacuation of what Gilman calls "sex attraction" in order to miti-

24. Charlotte Perkins Gilman, *The Living of Charlotte Perkins Gilman,* 154. See also Lois Magner, "Darwinism and the Woman Question," in *Critical Essays on Charlotte Perkins Gilman,* ed. Joanne Karpinski (New York: Maximillan, 1992).

25. See Cynthia Eagle Russett, *Sexual Science: The Victorian Construction of Womanhood* (Cambridge: Harvard University Press, 1989).

26. Herbert Spencer, *First Principles of a New System of Biology* (New York: Appleton, 1864), 516.

27. Gilman, *His Religion and Hers: A Study of the Faith of Our Fathers and the Work of Our Mothers.* (1923; reprint, Westport, Conn.: Hyperion Press, 1976), v.

gate the problems that could arise when young girls adorned themselves for male desire. She writes, "The more widely the sexes are differentiated, the more forcibly they are attracted to each other . . . so as to retard and confuse race-distinction . . . and seriously injure the race."[28] In other words, female sexuality, and more specifically, noneugenic sex, was what she perceived as one of the greatest problems of modernity. She argues: "We, as a race, manifest an excessive sex attraction, followed by its excessive indulgence; an excess which tends to pervert and exhaust desire as well as to injure reproduction."[29] For Gilman, via Ward, neither work nor education damaged women's reproductive abilities; rather, sexual pleasure itself did. For this reason, *The Crux* characterizes its (pointedly female) doctors as the ideal citizens of a new republic. Where "The Yellow Wallpaper" portrays heterosexual marriage as a catalyst for female hysteria and bad mothering, *The Crux* argues that eugenic unions are the genesis of a fit and vigorous national identity.

Yet while *The Crux* never explicitly addresses same-sex desire, there are moments when desire does circulate in the narrative through women's relationships in ways that seem to enact an exception to Gilman's anxiety over sexual attachment more generally. This should prove an interesting and complicated study for scholars of queer theory who may want to examine the novel's erotic investments, such as the affections exchanged between Vivian and most of the central female characters in the novel (Dr. Bellair, Adele St. Cloud, and her best friend Susie).[30] There are also significant biographical connections between the narrative and Gilman's own relationship with the aforementioned Adeline Knapp during the period that Gilman was managing a boarding house in California. *The Crux* thus poses significant questions for scholars and readers of queer texts: What happens when same-sex sexual desire surfaces in narratives despite expressed authorial intent, and how do the terms of sexuality at times transect conservative U.S. racial, nationalist, and gender discourses?

28. Gilman, *Women and Economics,* 31.

29. Gilman, *Women and Economics,* 32.

30. I owe this insight to one of the anonymous readers of Duke University Press, who also pointed out to me the significance of the character whom Vivian eventually marries, Dr. Hale, and his "successive relay of boys."

The marriage of feminism and eugenics in *The Crux* is not exceptional, but rather indicative of feminist reform campaigns during this period in which self-proclaimed feminists like Gilman, Margaret Sanger, Emma Goldman, and Victoria Woodhull advocated for sexual and economic freedom, reproductive necessity, and eugenic discipline simultaneously. Part of their agenda was to promote sex education at younger ages. Other efforts involved the push for safe and legal birth control, and, in turn, a campaign to convince poor women to use it. Finally, more drastic measures included a program of "negative eugenics": legal segregation and sterilization of "the unfit." At stake in these efforts was either the protection of the family from physical and "moral contagion" or the protection of the nation from the onslaught of "degenerate" children. As Goldman put it, denying women access to birth control would "legally encourage the increase of paupers, epileptics, dipsomaniacs, cripples, criminals, and degenerates."[31] Or, as Sanger declared: "More children from the fit, less children from the unfit."[32]

One major outcome of their advocacy in this area was the U.S. Supreme Court case *Buck v. Bell,* which arose in 1925 when Carrie Buck was committed to the Virginia Colony for Epileptics and Feeble-minded and ordered to be sterilized. In 1927 the case was carried to the U.S. Supreme Court where the order was upheld. The decision stated that sterilization on eugenic grounds was within the power of the state and that it did not constitute cruel or unusual punishment. When handing down the decision, Justice Oliver Wendell Holmes wrote, "It is better for all the world if instead of waiting to execute degenerate offspring for crime or to let them starve for their imbecility, society can prevent those who are manifestly unfit from continuing their kind." By 1930, some 30,000 women had been sterilized on eugenic grounds under the purview of this decision.[33] *The Crux* may be taken as emblematic of this cultural moment, for it indexes the post-Darwinist panic over "race suicide" which laid

31. Emma Goldman, *Mother Earth,* vol. II (1916), 459.
32. Quoted in Daniel Kevles, *In the Name of Eugenics: Genetics and the Uses of Human Heredity* (Cambridge: Harvard University Press, 1995), 90.
33. Ibid., 94.

emphasis on the duty of upper-class Anglo-Saxon women to reproduce for the sake of the survival of a healthy citizenry.

The concerns over degeneration in the United States may seem odd in a cultural climate that tends to be characterized by technological, urban, and economic progress. The reassuring grant of social progression, however, was always unsettled in practice. As the rapid expansion and commercialization of the nation's urban centers facilitated women's entry into and circulation within a proliferation of public spheres, as workers and consumers, tensions arose over the changing character of "femininity," over how to protect "innocent" youth from modern perversity or how to encourage sociobiological responsibility in the face of competing sexual, social, and economic possibilities.[34]

In *The Crux,* these tensions play themselves out as a heterosexual romance gone awry. In the company of her mentor, Dr. Jane Bellair, and her close friend, Adele St. Cloud, Vivian's repressed longings turn outward: both her desires and the prospects for her future are mediated through her vaguely eroticized relationships to each of these women and through a struggle between the paradigms of romance and medical realism that they each represent. Adele St. Cloud encourages and educates Vivian in the sphere of romance; Dr. Bellair teaches her lessons of eugenic responsibility. At first, it is Vivian's relationship with Adele St. Cloud, who is always "clothed in soft, clinging fabrics with a misty, veiled effect to them," that mediates (or clouds) Vivian's experience of her body. In preparation for a coed dance, Adele dresses Vivian in "a gown of white" with "fairy wings of lace" and "a scarf about her white neck," placing a string of pearls on her "white throat." Vivian looks in the mirror and sees the effects of her "brilliant attire": "Erect, slender, graceful, the long lines of her long body draped in soft white" complemented "her head poised on its white column, rising from the shimmering lace." Vivian's first encounter with her body repeats a familiar narrative. Adele St. Cloud's "sentimental education" foments a particular version of fem-

34. See Margaret Jones, "Woman's Body, Worker's Right: Feminist Self-Fashioning and the Fight for Birth Control, 1898–1917," in *American Bodies: Cultural Histories of the Physique,* ed. Tim Armstrong (New York: New York University Press, 1996).

inine selfhood predicated on the seduction novel. Gilman replays the genre with her own version of the young, middle-class, white woman's treacherous coming-of-age story. Vivian's sexual awakening is accompanied by sexual danger, because her would-be dance partner-cum-husband, the aforementioned Morton, has syphilis. But the intense repetition of Vivian's white accessories together with the emphasis on her white skin also seems to signal the racial requirement of this narrative. Vivian is, in the most banal terms, "white": at once a paragon of sexual virtue and racial "purity."

However, this is the kind of female-female exchange that Gilman argued against. If this scene of sexual awakening plays an important part in Vivian's progress facilitating a set of "erections" and "risings"—a progression rendered in both sexual and evolutionary terms—it is nonetheless a version of feminine selfhood overdetermined by the trappings of the conventional romance novel and a culture of conspicuous consumption. Vivian's body in this scene is a decorated building, a Greek "column" of feminine beauty vulnerable to sexually transmitted disease. This type of "consuming female," Gilman argues, "creates a market for sensuous decoration and personal ornament, for all that is luxurious and enervating," by which "the over-sexed woman . . . hinders and perverts the economic development of the world."[35]

For Vivian, it is the activity of work and her physical education that inaugurates the kind of self-transformation that Gilman advocates. In addition to starting up her own kindergarten, Vivian begins to teach exercise to "a class of rather delicate children and young girls." Vivian's new career enables her to move from the domestic sphere into the sphere of activity and work as a professional teacher. The narrative tracks her progression from a New England lifestyle marked by boredom and a sense of uselessness into a position of economic independence. Exercising also expands Vivian's mental health by providing her with "a new fresh interest in her own body and the use of it." Instead of displaying her body as a sentimental ornament for the purpose of male attraction, she discovers it as both a pedagogical tool to aid other sickly young girls and as a matter of personal

35. Gilman, *Women and Economics,* 120–21.

interest—for it is precisely Vivian's ability to teach others about their bodies that allows her to experience knowledge of her own body.

Gilman positions this active, healthy body that Dr. Bellair encourages in direct contradistinction to the immobility of feminine display that Vivian first encounters with Adele St. Cloud. Her new, "fresh" body enables a better self and a healthier life, above and beyond the dangers of sentimental love. She soon "arose and quietly set to work arranging her room in its new capacity of hers only." Vivian's growing understanding of her property—that which is "hers only"—signals her movement toward a model of feminine autonomy. The evolution of femininity that Gilman proposes involves carving out a space disaggregated from either a dominating male economy or an economy of female sentiment.

It is also significant that the specter of sexual disease haunts *The Crux*. Morton Elder, Vivian's potential lover, is "a motherless boy" with "no good woman's influence about." Dr. Jane Bellair tries to warn her good friend Vivian of his illness: "You must not marry Morton Elder. I know he has syphilis . . . one of the most terrible diseases known to us; highly contagious and . . . hereditary." Here, the logic of syphilis has been borrowed to establish a domain of masculine sexual deviance in binary opposition to the healthy feminine regime that Gilman's work imagines.[36] The novel codes syphilis as a danger not because it is a sexually transmitted disease but because it is a sexually transmitted disease that is also "hereditary," a catalyst to familial, cultural, and national degeneration. As I have already suggested, stopping the force of degeneration means that mothers, burdened with the cleansing of the future, must eschew sexuality for reproductivity; they must substitute a desire to reproduce for sexual feeling. In Dr. Bellair's role as Vivian's caretaker, the regulatory ideals of eugenic science register as domestic affect. This new affective register—which casts sentimental bonds not within the terms of domestic feeling but rather of eugenic prescription—proposes a strategy for imagining collective feminist struggle and "hy-

36. For a thorough account of the anxieties over syphilis in the United States, see Alan Brandt, *No Magic Bullet: A Social History of Venereal Disease in the United States since 1880* (New York: Oxford University Press, 1987).

gienic" social progress simultaneously. It also hints at the major function of this strategy: it is enacted in the service of the formation of a new kind of family, one consisting primarily of women and embedded in scientific decree. The novel's model of motherhood, in its accumulation of imperatives for self-management and in its racialist impulses, demonstrates how movements that we might commonly take as progressive—such as feminism—often employ or are constituted by other discourses—such as biology—to exert regulatory, prohibitive functions.[37]

But readers of *The Crux* should not necessarily employ it as a way to repudiate the earlier feminist reclamation of Gilman's work that posed such a crucial challenge to the literary canon. Instead, it can be seen as a significant text that enables an account of how the histories of our feminisms are not politically transparent but fraught with a complex and dialectical history of promise and damage. In this instance, the driving forces of white progressive feminism helped instantiate and inform what we might think of as a new version of liberal humanism in which the mother acts as ideal civic progenitor. In a move from an ideal of self-governance to an ideal of eugenic familialism, a public valorization of motherhood emerges in ways that parallel—and indeed are grounded in—the tenets of popularized evolutionism and eugenics.

UNLIKE OTHER TEXTS that have been pored over by contemporary literary critics in Gilman's oeuvre, *The Crux* has never been given the attention it merits. Perhaps because of the size of its press, or perhaps because it was easy to overlook amongst Gilman's prolific output of writing, *The Crux* was released without a flourish and apparently without comment from the mainstream literary community. Given that the rest of her considerable corpus has proven so valuable to the thinking-through of American literary history and early feminism, this text's relative anonymity is rather surprising. One would hope that the reissue of *The Crux* will constitute one more step toward a

37. For other contemporaneous novels that deal directly, indirectly, or metaphorically with themes of motherhood and/or eugenics, see Kate Chopin, *The Awakening* (1899), Edith Wharton, *The House of Mirth* (1905), Edith Summers Kelley, *Weeds* (1923), and Pauline Hopkins, *Contending Forces* (1900).

serious (re)appraisal of heretofore overlooked contours of Western racial and feminist discourses. When Vivian herself first meets Dr. Jane Bellair, she faces the ambivalence that always accompanies change: "Vivian liked her, yet felt afraid, a slight, shivering hesitancy as before a too cold bath, a subtle sense that this breezy woman, strong, cheerful, full of new ideas, if not ideals, and radiating actual power, power used and enjoyed, might in some way change the movement of her life." Perhaps it is not too ambitious to suggest that *The Crux* might in some way change contemporary accounts of both Gilman's work and early feminism.

Dana Seitler, 2002

THE CRUX

AUTHOR'S PREFACE

This story is, first, for young women to read; second, for young men to read; after that, for anybody who wants to. Anyone who doubts its facts and figures is referred to "Social Diseases and Marriage," by Dr. Prince Morrow, or to "Hygiene and Morality," by Miss Lavinia Dock, a trained nurse of long experience.

Some will hold that the painful facts disclosed are unfit for young girls to know. Young girls are precisely the ones who must know them, in order that they may protect themselves and their children to come. The time to know of danger is before it is too late to avoid it.

If some say "Innocence is the greatest charm of young girls," the answer is, "What good does it do them?"

Who should know but the woman?—The young wife-to-be?
    Whose whole life hangs on the choice;
To her the ruin, the misery;
    To her, the deciding voice.

Who should know but the woman?—The mother-to-be?
    Guardian, Giver, and Guide;
If she may not foreknow, forejudge and foresee,
    What safety has childhood beside?

Who should know but the woman?—The girl in her youth?
    The hour of the warning is then,
That, strong in her knowledge and free in her truth,
    She may build a new race of new men.

1

THE BACK WAY

Along the same old garden path,
Sweet with the same old flowers;
Under the lilacs, darkly dense,
The easy gate in the backyard fence—
Those unforgotten hours!

The "Foote Girls" were bustling along Margate Street with an air of united purpose that was unusual with them. Miss Rebecca wore her black silk cloak, by which it might be seen that "a call" was toward. Miss Josie, the thin sister, and Miss Sallie, the fat one, were more hastily attired. They were persons of less impressiveness than Miss Rebecca, as was tacitly admitted by their more familiar nicknames, a concession never made by the older sister.

Even Miss Rebecca was hurrying a little, for her, but the others were swifter and more impatient.

"Do come on, Rebecca. Anybody'd think you were eighty instead of fifty!" said Miss Sallie.

"There's Mrs. Williams going in! I wonder if she's heard already. Do hurry!" urged Miss Josie.

But Miss Rebecca, being concerned about her dignity, would not allow herself to be hustled, and the three proceeded in irregular order under the high-arched elms and fence-topping syringas of the small New England town toward the austere home of Mr. Samuel Lane.

It was a large, uncompromising, square, white house, planted starkly in the close-cut grass. It had no porch for summer lounging, no front gate for evening dalliance, no path-bordering beds of flowers from which to pluck a hasty offering or more redundant tribute. The fragrance which surrounded it came from the back yard, or over the fences of neighbors; the trees which waved greenly about it were the trees of other people. Mr. Lane had but two trees, one on each side of the straight and narrow path, evenly placed between house and sidewalk—evergreens.

Mrs. Lane received them amiably; the minister's new wife, Mrs. Williams, was proving a little difficult to entertain. She was from Cambridge, Mass., and emanated a restrained consciousness of that fact. Mr. Lane rose stiffly and greeted them. He did not like the Foote girls, not having the usual American's share of the sense of humor. He had no enjoyment of the town joke, as old as they were, that "the three of them made a full yard;" and had frowned down as a profane impertinent the man—a little sore under some effect of gossip—who had amended it with "make an 'ell, I say."

Safely seated in their several rocking chairs, and severally rocking them, the Misses Foote burst forth, as was their custom, in simultaneous, though by no means identical remarks.

"I suppose you've heard about Morton Elder?"

"What do you think Mort Elder's been doing now?"

"We've got bad news for poor Miss Elder!"

Mrs. Lane was intensely interested. Even Mr. Lane showed signs of animation.

"I'm not surprised," he said.

"He's done it now," opined Miss Josie with conviction. "I always said Rella Elder was spoiling that boy."

"It's too bad—after all she's done for him! He always was a scamp!" Thus Miss Sallie.

"I've been afraid of it all along," Miss Rebecca was saying, her voice booming through the lighter tones of her sisters. "I always said he'd never get through college."

"But who is Morton Elder, and what has he done?" asked Mrs. Williams as soon as she could be heard.

This lady now proved a most valuable asset. She was so new to the town, and had been so immersed in the suddenly widening range of her unsalaried duties as "minister's wife," that she had never even heard of Morton Elder.

A new resident always fans the languishing flame of local conversation. The whole shopworn stock takes on a fresh lustre, topics long trampled flat in much discussion lift their heads anew, opinions one scarce dared to repeat again become almost authoritative, old stories flourish freshly, acquiring new detail and more vivid color.

Mrs. Lane, seizing her opportunity while the sisters gasped a momentary amazement at anyone's not knowing the town scapegrace, and taking advantage of her position as old friend and near neighbor of the family under discussion, swept into the field under such headway that even the Foote girls remained silent perforce; surcharged, however, and holding their breaths in readiness to burst forth at the first opening.

"He's the nephew—orphan nephew—of Miss Elder—who lives right back of us—our yards touch—we've always been friends—went to school together, Rella's never married—she teaches, you know—and her brother—he owned the home—it's all hers now, he died all of a sudden and left two children—Morton and Susie. Mort was about seven years old and Susie just a baby. He's been an awful cross—but she just idolizes him—she's spoiled him, I tell her."

Mrs. Lane had to breathe, and even the briefest pause left her stranded to wait another chance. The three social benefactors proceeded to distribute their information in a clattering torrent. They sought to inform Mrs. Williams in especial, of numberless details of the early life and education of their subject, matters which would have been treated more appreciatively if they had not been blessed with the later news; and, at the same time, each was seeking for a more dramatic emphasis to give this last supply of incident with due effect.

No regular record is possible where three persons pour forth statement and comment in a rapid, tumultuous stream, interrupted by cross currents of heated contradiction, and further varied by the exclamations and protests of three hearers, or at least, of two; for the one man present soon relapsed into disgusted silence.

Mrs. Williams, turning a perplexed face from one to the other, inwardly condemning the darkening flood of talk, yet conscious of a sinful pleasure in it, and anxious as a guest, *and* a minister's wife, to be most amiable, felt like one watching three kinetescopes at once. She saw, in confused pictures of blurred and varying outline, Orella Elder, the young New England girl, only eighteen, already a "school ma'am," suddenly left with two children to bring up, and doing it, as best she could. She saw the boy, momentarily changing, in his shuttlecock flight from mouth to mouth, through pale shades of open mischief to the black and scarlet of hinted sin, the terror of the neighborhood, the darling of his aunt, clever, audacious, scandalizing the quiet town.

"Boys are apt to be mischievous, aren't they?" she suggested when it was possible.

"He's worse than mischievous," Mr. Lane assured her sourly. "There's a mean streak in that family."

"That's on his mother's side," Mrs. Lane hastened to add. "She was a queer girl—came from New York."

The Foote girls began again, with rich profusion of detail, their voices rising shrill, one above the other, and playing together at their full height like emulous fountains.

"We ought not to judge, you know;" urged Mrs. Williams. "What do you say he's really done?"

Being sifted, it appeared that this last and most terrible performance was to go to "the city" with a group of "the worst boys of college," to get undeniably drunk, to do some piece of mischief. (Here was great license in opinion, and in contradiction.)

"*Anyway* he's to be suspended!" said Miss Rebecca with finality.

"Suspended!" Miss Josie's voice rose in scorn. "*Expelled!* They said he was expelled."

"In disgrace!" added Miss Sallie.

Vivian Lane sat in the back room at the window, studying in the lingering light of the long June evening. At least, she appeared to be studying. Her tall figure was bent over her books, but the dark eyes blazed under their delicate level brows, and her face flushed and paled with changing feelings.

She had heard—who, in the same house, could escape hearing the Misses Foote?—and had followed the torrent of description, hearsay, surmise and allegation with an interest that was painful in its intensity.

"It's a *shame!*" she whispered under her breath. "A *shame!* And nobody to stand up for him!"

She half rose to her feet as if to do it herself, but sank back irresolutely.

A fresh wave of talk rolled forth.

"It'll half kill his aunt."

"Poor Miss Elder! I don't know what she'll do!"

"I don't know what *he'll* do. He can't go back to college."

"He'll have to go to work."

"I'd like to know where—nobody'd hire him in this town."

The girl could bear it no longer. She came to the door, and there, as they paused to speak to her, her purpose ebbed again.

"My daughter, Vivian, Mrs. Williams," said her mother; and the other callers greeted her familiarly.

"You'd better finish your lessons, Vivian," Mr. Lane suggested.

"I have, father," said the girl, and took a chair by the minister's wife. She had a vague feeling that if she were there, they would not talk so about Morton Elder.

Mrs. Williams hailed the interruption gratefully. She liked the slender girl with the thoughtful eyes and pretty, rather pathetic mouth, and sought to draw her out. But her questions soon led to unfortunate results.

"You are going to college, I suppose?" she presently inquired; and Vivian owned that it was the desire of her heart.

"Nonsense!" said her father. "Stuff and nonsense, Vivian! You're not going to college."

The Foote girls now burst forth in voluble agreement with Mr. Lane. His wife was evidently of the same mind; and Mrs. Williams plainly regretted her question. But Vivian mustered courage enough to make a stand, strengthened perhaps by the depth of the feeling which had brought her into the room.

"I don't know why you're all so down on a girl's going to college. Eve Marks has gone, and Mary Spring is going—and both the Austin girls. Everybody goes now."

"I know one girl that won't," was her father's incisive comment, and her mother said quietly, "A girl's place is at home—'till she marries."

"Suppose I don't want to marry?" said Vivian.

"Don't talk nonsense," her father answered. "Marriage is a woman's duty."

"What do you want to do?" asked Miss Josie in the interests of further combat. "Do you want to be a doctor, like Jane Bellair?"

"I should like to very much indeed," said the girl with quiet intensity. "I'd like to be a doctor in a babies' hospital."

"More nonsense," said Mr. Lane. "Don't talk to me about that woman! You attend to your studies, and then to your home duties, my dear."

The talk rose anew, the three sisters contriving all to agree with Mr. Lane in his opinions about college, marriage and Dr. Bellair, yet to disagree violently among themselves.

Mrs. Williams rose to go, and in the lull that followed the liquid note of a whippoorwill met the girl's quick ear. She quietly slipped out, unnoticed.

The Lane's home stood near the outer edge of the town, with an outlook across wide meadows and soft wooded hills. Behind, their long garden backed on that of Miss Orella Elder, with a connecting gate in the gray board fence. Mrs. Lane had grown up here. The house belonged to her mother, Mrs. Servilla Pettigrew, though that able lady was seldom in it, preferring to make herself useful among two growing sets of grandchildren.

Miss Elder was Vivian's favorite teacher. She was a careful and conscientious instructor, and the girl was a careful and conscientious scholar; so they got on admirably together; indeed, there was a real affection between them. And just as the young Laura Pettigrew had played with the younger Orella Elder, so Vivian had played with little Susie Elder, Miss Orella's orphan niece. Susie regarded the older girl with worshipful affection, which was not at all unpleasant to an emotional young creature with unemotional parents, and no brothers or sisters of her own.

Moreover, Susie was Morton's sister.

The whippoorwill's cry sounded again through the soft June night. Vivian came quickly down the garden path between the bordering beds of sweet alyssum and mignonette. A dew-wet rose brushed against her hand. She broke it off, pricking her fingers, and hastily fastened it in the bosom of her white frock.

Large old lilac bushes hung over the dividing fence, a thick mass of honeysuckle climbed up by the gate and mingled with them, spreading over to a pear tree on the Lane side. In this fragrant, hidden corner was a rough seat, and from it a boy's hand reached out and seized the girl's, drawing her down beside him. She drew away from him as far as the seat allowed.

"Oh Morton!" she said. "What have you done?"

Morton was sulky.

"Now Vivian, are you down on me too? I thought I had one friend."

"You ought to tell me," she said more gently. "How can I be your friend if I don't know the facts? They are saying perfectly awful things."

"Who are?"

"Why—the Foote girls—everybody."

"Oh those old maids aren't everybody, I assure you. You see, Vivian, you live right here in this old oyster of a town—and you make mountains out of molehills like everybody else. A girl of your intelligence ought to know better."

She drew a great breath of relief. "Then you haven't—done it?"

"Done what? What's all this mysterious talk anyhow? The prisoner has a right to know what he's charged with before he commits himself."

The girl was silent, finding it difficult to begin.

"Well, out with it. What do they say I did?" He picked up a long dry twig and broke it, gradually, into tiny, half-inch bits.

"They say you—went to the city—with a lot of the worst boys in college—"

"Well? Many persons go to the city every day. That's no crime, surely. As for 'the worst boys in college,' "—he laughed scornfully—"I suppose those old ladies think if a fellow smokes a cigarette or says 'darn' he's a tough. They're mighty nice fellows, that bunch—most of 'em. Got some ginger in 'em, that's all. What else?"

"They say—you drank."

"O ho! Said I got drunk, I warrant! Well—we did have a skate on that time, I admit!" And he laughed as if this charge were but a familiar joke.

"Why Morton Elder! I think it is a—disgrace!"

"Pshaw, Vivian!—You ought to have more sense. All the fellows get gay once in a while. A college isn't a young ladies' seminary."

He reached out and got hold of her hand again, but she drew it away.

"There was something else," she said.

"What was it?" he questioned sharply. "What did they say?"

But she would not satisfy him—perhaps could not.

"I should think you'd be ashamed, to make your aunt so much trouble. They said you were suspended—or—*expelled!*"

He shrugged his big shoulders and threw away the handful of broken twigs.

"That's true enough—I might as well admit that."

"Oh, *Morton!*—I didn't believe it. *Expelled!*"

"Yes, expelled—turned down—thrown out—fired! And I'm glad of it." He leaned back against the fence and whistled very softly through his teeth.

"Sh! Sh!" she urged. "Please!"

He was quiet.

"But Morton—what are you going to do?—Won't it spoil your career?"

"No, my dear little girl, it will not!" said he. "On the contrary, it will be the making of me. I tell you, Vivian, I'm sick to death of this town of maiden ladies—and 'good family men.' I'm sick of being fussed over for ever and ever, and having wristers and mufflers knitted for me—and being told to put on my rubbers! There's no fun in this old clamshell—this kitchen-midden of a town—and I'm going to quit it."

He stood up and stretched his long arms. "I'm going to quit it for good and all."

The girl sat still, her hands gripping the seat on either side.

"Where are you going?" she asked in a low voice.

"I'm going west—clear out west. I've been talking with Aunt Rella about it. Dr. Bellair'll help me to a job, she thinks. She's awful cut up, of course. I'm sorry she feels bad—but she needn't, I tell her. I shall do better there than I ever should have here. I know a fellow that left college—his father failed—and he went into business and made two thousand dollars in a year. I always wanted to take up business—you know that!"

She knew it—he had talked of it freely before they had argued and persuaded him into the college life. She knew, too, how his aunt's hopes all centered in him, and in his academic honors and future professional life. "Business," to his aunt's mind, was a necessary evil, which could at best be undertaken only after a "liberal education."

"When are you going," she asked at length.

"Right off—to-morrow."

She gave a little gasp.

"That's what I was whippoorwilling about—I knew I'd get no other chance to talk to vou—I wanted to say good-by, you know."

The girl sat silent, struggling not to cry. He dropped beside her, stole an arm about her waist, and felt her tremble.

"Now, Viva, don't you go and cry! I'm sorry—I really am sorry—to make *you* feel bad."

This was too much for her, and she sobbed frankly.

"Oh, Morton! How could you! How could you!—And now you've got to go away!"

"There now—don't cry—sh!—they'll hear you."

She did hush at that.

"And don't feel so bad—I'll come back some time—to see you."

"No, you won't!" she answered with sudden fierceness. "You'll just go—and stay—and I never shall see you again!"

He drew her closer to him. "And do you care—so much—Viva?"

"Of course, I care!" she said, "Haven't we always been friends, the best of friends?"

"Yes—you and Aunt Rella have been about all I had," he admitted with a cheerful laugh. "I hope I'll make more friends out yonder. But Viva"—his hand pressed closer—"is it only—friends?"

She took fright at once and drew away from him. "You mustn't do that, Morton!"

"Do what?" A shaft of moonlight shone on his teasing face. "What am I doing?" he said.

It is difficult—it is well nigh impossible—for a girl to put a name to certain small cuddlings not in themselves terrifying, nor even unpleasant, but which she obscurely feels to be wrong.

Viva flushed and was silent—he could see the rich color flood her face.

"Come now—don't be hard on a fellow!" he urged. "I shan't

see you again in ever so long. You'll forget all about me before a year's over."

She shook her head, still silent.

"Won't you speak to me—Viva?"

"I wish—" She could not find the words she wanted. "Oh, I wish you—wouldn't!"

"Wouldn't what, Girlie? Wouldn't go away? Sorry to disoblige—but I have to. There's no place for me here."

The girl felt the sad truth of that.

"Aunt Rella will get used to it after a while. I'll write to her—I'll make lots of money—and come back in a few years—astonish you all!—Meanwhile—kiss me good-by, Viva!"

She drew back shyly. She had never kissed him. She had never in her life kissed any man younger than an uncle.

"No, Morton—you mustn't—" She shrank away into the shadow.

But, there was no great distance to shrink to, and his strong arms soon drew her close again.

"Suppose you never see me again," he said. "Then you'll wish you hadn't been so stiff about it."

She thought of this dread possibility with a sudden chill of horror, and while she hesitated, he took her face between his hands and kissed her on the mouth.

Steps were heard coming down the path.

"They're on," he said with a little laugh. "Good-by, Viva!"

He vaulted the fence and was gone.

"What are you doing here, Vivian?" demanded her father.

"I was saying good-by to Morton," she answered with a sob.

"You ought to be ashamed of yourself—philandering out here in the middle of the night with that scapegrace! Come in the house and go to bed at once—it's ten o'clock."

Bowing to this confused but almost equally incriminating chronology, she followed him in, meekly enough as to her outward seeming, but inwardly in a state of stormy tumult.

She had been kissed!

Her father's stiff back before her could not blot out the radiant, melting moonlight, the rich sweetness of the flowers, the tender, soft, June night.

"You go to bed," said he once more. "I'm ashamed of you."

"Yes, father," she answered.

Her little room, when at last she was safely in it and had shut the door and put a chair against it—she had no key—seemed somehow changed.

She lit the lamp and stood looking at herself in the mirror. Her eyes were star-bright. Her cheeks flamed softly. Her mouth looked guilty and yet glad.

She put the light out and went to the window, kneeling there, leaning out in the fragrant stillness, trying to arrange in her mind this mixture of grief, disapproval, shame and triumph.

When the Episcopal church clock struck eleven, she went to bed in guilty haste, but not to sleep.

For a long time she lay there watching the changing play of moonlight on the floor.

She felt almost as if she were married.

2

BAINVILLE EFFECTS

Lockstep, handcuffs, ankle-ball-and-chain,
Dulltoil and dreary food and drink;
Small cell, cold cell, narrow bed and hard;
High wall, thick wall, window iron-barred;
Stone-paved, stone-pent little prison yard—
Young hearts weary of monotony and pain,
Young hearts weary of reiterant refrain:
"They say—they do—what will people think?"

At the two front windows of their rather crowded little parlor sat Miss Rebecca and Miss Josie Foote, Miss Sallie being out on a foraging expedition—marketing, as it were, among their neighbors to collect fresh food for thought.

A tall, slender girl in brown passed on the opposite walk.

"I should think Vivian Lane would get tired of wearing brown," said Miss Rebecca.

"I don't know why she should," her sister promptly protested, "it's a good enough wearing color, and becoming to her."

"She could afford to have more variety," said Miss Rebecca. "The Lanes are mean enough about some things, but I know they'd like to have her dress better. She'll never get married in the world."

"I don't know why not. She's only twenty-five—and good-looking."

"Good-looking! That's not everything. Plenty of girls marry that are not good-looking—and plenty of good-looking girls stay single."

"Plenty of homely ones, too. Rebecca," said Miss Josie, with meaning. Miss Rebecca certainly was not handsome. "Going to the library, of course!" she pursued presently. "That girl reads all the time."

"So does her grandmother. I see her going and coming from that library every day almost."

"Oh, well—she reads stories and things like that. Sallie goes pretty often and she notices. We use that library enough, goodness knows, but they are there every day. Vivian Lane reads the queerest things—doctor's books and works on pedagoggy."

"Godgy," said Miss Rebecca, "not goggy." And as her sister ignored this correction, she continued: "They might as well have let her go to college when she was so set on it."

"College! I don't believe she'd have learned as much in any college, from what I hear of 'em, as she has in all this time at home." The Foote girls had never entertained a high opinion of extensive culture.

"I don't see any use in a girl's studying so much," said Miss Rebecca with decision.

"Nor I," agreed Miss Josie. "Men don't like learned women."

"They don't seem to always like those that aren't learned, either," remarked Miss Rebecca with a pleasant sense of retribution for that remark about "homely ones."

The tall girl in brown had seen the two faces at the windows opposite, and had held her shoulders a little straighter as she turned the corner.

"Nine years this Summer since Morton Elder went West," murmured Miss Josie, reminiscently. "I shouldn't wonder if Vivian had stayed single on his account."

"Nonsense!" her sister answered sharply. "She's not that kind. She's not popular with men, that's all. She's too intellectual."

"She ought to be in the library instead of Sue Elder," Miss Josie suggested. "She's far more competent. Sue's a feather-headed little thing."

"She seems to give satisfaction so far. If the trustees are pleased with her, there's no reason for you to complain that I see," said Miss Rebecca with decision.

VIVIAN LANE WAITED at the library desk with an armful of books to take home. She had her card, her mother's and her father's—

all utilized. Her grandmother kept her own card—and her own counsel.

The pretty assistant librarian, withdrawing herself with some emphasis from the unnecessary questions of a too gallant old gentleman, came to attend her.

"You *have* got a load," she said, scribbling complex figures with one end of her hammer-headed pencil, and stamping violet dates with the other. She whisked out the pale blue slips from the lid pockets, dropped them into their proper openings in the desk and inserted the cards in their stead with delicate precision.

"Can't you wait a bit and go home with me?" she asked. "I'll help you carry them."

"No, thanks. I'm not going right home."

"You're going to see your Saint—I know!" said Miss Susie, tossing her bright head. "I'm jealous, and you know it."

"Don't be a goose, Susie! You know you're my very best friend, but—she's different."

"I should think she was different!" Susie sharply agreed. "And you've been 'different' ever since she came."

"I hope so," said Vivian gravely. "Mrs. St. Cloud brings out one's very best and highest. I wish you liked her better, Susie."

"I like you," Susie answered. "You bring out my 'best and highest'—if I've got any. She don't. She's like a lovely, faint, bright—bubble! I want to prick it!"

Vivian smiled down upon her.

"You bad little mouse!" she said. "Come, give me the books."

"Leave them with me, and I'll bring them in the car." Susie looked anxious to make amends for her bit of blasphemy.

"All right, dear. Thank you. I'll be home by that time, probably."

IN THE STREET she stopped before a little shop where papers and magazines were sold.

"I believe Father'd like the new Centurion," she said to herself, and got it for him, chatting a little with the one-armed man who kept the place. She stopped again at a small florist's and bought a little bag of bulbs.

"Your mother's forgotten about those, I guess," said Mrs. Crothers, the florist's wife, "but they'll do just as well now. Lucky you thought of them before it got too late in the season. Bennie was awfully pleased with that red and blue pencil you gave him, Miss Lane."

Vivian walked on. A child ran out suddenly from a gate and seized upon her.

"Aren't you coming in to see me—ever?" she demanded.

Vivian stooped and kissed her.

"Yes, dear, but not to-night. How's that dear baby getting on?"

"She's better," said the little girl. "Mother said thank you—lots of times. Wait a minute—"

The child fumbled in Vivian's coat pocket with a mischievous upward glance, fished out a handful of peanuts, and ran up the path laughing while the tall girl smiled down upon her lovingly.

A long-legged boy was lounging along the wet sidewalk. Vivian caught up with him and he joined her with eagerness.

"Good evening, Miss Lane. Say—are you coming to the club to-morrow night?"

She smiled cordially.

"Of course I am, Johnny. I wouldn't disappoint my boys for anything—nor myself, either."

They walked on together chatting until, at the minister's house, she bade him a cheery "good-night."

Mrs. St. Cloud was at the window pensively watching the western sky. She saw the girl coming and let her in with a tender, radiant smile—a lovely being in a most unlovely room.

There was a chill refinement above subdued confusion in that Cambridge-Bainville parlor, where the higher culture of the second Mrs. Williams, superimposed upon the lower culture of the first, as that upon the varying tastes of a combined ancestry, made the place somehow suggestive of excavations at Abydos.

It was much the kind of parlor Vivian had been accustomed to from childhood, but Mrs. St. Cloud was of a type quite new to her. Clothed in soft, clinging fabrics, always with a misty, veiled effect to them, wearing pale amber, large, dull stones of uncertain shapes, and slender chains that glittered here and there among her scarfs and laces, sinking gracefully among deep cushions, even able to sink gracefully into a common Bainville chair—this beautiful woman had captured the girl's imagination from the first.

Clearly known, she was a sister of Mrs. Williams, visiting indefinitely. Vaguely—and very frequently—hinted, her husband had "left her," and "she did not believe in divorce." Against her background of dumb patience, he shone darkly forth as a Brute of unknown cruelties. Nothing against him would she ever say, and every young masculine heart yearned to make life brighter to the Ideal Woman, so strangely neglected; also some older ones. Her Young Men's Bible Class was the pride of Mr. Williams' heart and joy of such young men as the town possessed; most of Bainville's boys had gone.

"A wonderful uplifting influence," Mr. Williams called her, and refused to say anything, even when directly approached, as to "the facts" of her trouble. "It is an old story," he would say. "She bears up wonderfully. She sacrifices her life rather than her principles."

To Vivian, sitting now on a hassock at the lady's feet and looking up at her with adoring eyes, she was indeed a star, a saint, a cloud of mystery.

She reached out a soft hand, white, slender, delicately kept, wearing one thin gold ring, and stroked the girl's smooth hair. Vivian seized the hand and kissed it, blushing as she did so.

"You foolish child! Don't waste your young affection on an old lady like me."

"Old! You! You don't look as old as I do this minute!" said the girl with hushed intensity.

"Life wears on you, I'm afraid, my dear. . . . Do you ever hear from him?"

To no one else, not even to Susie, could Vivian speak of what now seemed the tragedy of her lost youth.

"No," said she. "Never now. He did write once or twice—at first."

"He writes to his aunt, of course?"

"Yes," said Vivian. "But not often. And he never—says anything."

"I understand. Poor child! You must be true, and wait." And the lady turned the thin ring on her finger. Vivian watched her in a passion of admiring tenderness.

"Oh, you understand!" she exclaimed. "You understand!"

"I understand, my dear," said Mrs. St. Cloud.

When Vivian reached her own gate she leaned her arms upon it and looked first one way and then the other, down the long, still street. The country was in sight at both ends—the low, monotonous, wooded hills that shut them in. It was all familiar, wearingly familiar. She had known it continuously for such part of her lifetime as was sensitive to landscape effects, and had at times a mad wish for an earthquake to change the outlines a little.

The infrequent trolley car passed just then and Sue Elder joined her, to take the short cut home through the Lane's yard.

"Here you are," she said cheerfully, "and here are the books."

Vivian thanked her.

"Oh, say—come in after supper, can't you? Aunt Rella's had another letter from Mort."

Vivian's sombre eyes lit up a little.

"How's he getting on? In the same business he was last year?" she asked with an elaborately cheerful air. Morton had seemed to change occupations oftener than he wrote letters.

"Yes, I believe so. I guess he's well. He never says much, you know. I don't think it's good for him out there—good for any boy." And Susie looked quite the older sister.

"What are they to do? They can't stay here."

"No, I suppose not—but we have to."

"Dr. Bellair didn't," remarked Vivian. "I like her—tremendously, don't you?" In truth, Dr. Bellair was already a close second to Mrs. St. Cloud in the girl's hero-worshipping heart.

"Oh, yes; she's splendid! Aunt Rella is so glad to have her with us. They have great times recalling their school days together. Aunty used to like her then, though she is five years older—but you'd never dream it. And I think she's real handsome."

"She's not beautiful," said Vivian, with decision, "but she's a lot better. Sue Elder, I wish—"

"Wish what?" asked her friend.

Sue put the books on the gate-post, and the two girls, arm in arm, walked slowly up and down.

Susie was a round, palely rosy little person, with a delicate face and soft, light hair waving fluffily about her small head. Vivian's hair was twice the length, but so straight and fine that its mass had no effect. She wore it in smooth plaits wound like a wreath from brow to nape.

After an understanding silence and a walk past three gates and back again, Vivian answered her.

"I wish I were in your shoes," she said.

"What do you mean—having the Doctor in the house?"

"No—I'd like that too; but I mean work to do—your position."

"Oh, the library! You needn't; it's horrid. I wish I were in your shoes, and had a father and mother to take care of me. I can tell you, it's no fun—having to be there just on time or get fined, and having to poke away all day with those phooty old ladies and tiresome children."

"But you're independent."

"Oh, yes, I'm independent. I have to be. Aunt Rella *could* take care of me, I suppose, but of course I wouldn't let her. And I dare say library work is better than school-teaching."

"What'll we be doing when we're forty, I wonder?" said Vivian, after another turn.

"Forty! Why I expect to be a grandma by that time," said Sue. She was but twenty-one, and forty looked a long way off to her.

"A grandma! And knit?" suggested Vivian.

"Oh, yes—baby jackets—and blankets—and socks—and little shawls. I love to knit," said Sue, cheerfully.

"But suppose you don't marry?" pursued her friend.

"Oh, but I shall marry—you see if I don't. Marriage"—here she carefully went inside the gate and latched it—"marriage is—a woman's duty!" And she ran up the path laughing.

Vivian laughed too, rather grimly, and slowly walked towards her own door.

The little sitting-room was hot, very hot; but Mr. Lane sat with his carpet-slippered feet on its narrow hearth with a shawl around him.

"Shut the door, Vivian!" he exclaimed irritably. "I'll never get over this cold if such draughts are let in on me."

"Why, it's not cold out, Father—and it's very close in here."

Mrs. Lane looked up from her darning. "You think it's close because you've come in from outdoors. Sit down—and don't fret your father; I'm real worried about him."

Mr. Lane coughed hollowly. He had become a little dry old man with gray, glassy eyes, and had been having colds in this fashion ever since Vivian could remember.

"Dr. Bellair says that the out-door air is the best medicine for a cold," remarked Vivian, as she took off her things.

"Dr. Bellair has not been consulted in this case," her father returned wheezingly. "I'm quite satisfied with my family physician. He's a man, at any rate."

"Save me from these women doctors!" exclaimed his wife.

Vivian set her lips patiently. She had long since learned how widely she differed from both father and mother, and preferred silence to dispute.

Mr. Lane was a plain, ordinary person, who spent most of a moderately useful life in the shoe business, from which he had of late withdrawn. Both he and his wife "had property" to a certain extent; and now lived peacefully on their income with neither fear nor hope, ambition nor responsibility to trouble them. The one thing they were yet anxious about was to see Vivian married, but this wish seemed to be no nearer to fulfillment for the passing years.

"I don't know what the women are thinking of, these days," went on the old gentleman, putting another shovelful of coal on the fire with a careful hand. "Doctors and lawyers and even ministers, some of 'em! The Lord certainly set down a woman's duty pretty plain—she was to cleave unto her husband!"

"Some women have no husbands to cleave to, Father."

"They'd have husbands fast enough if they'd behave themselves," he answered. "No man's going to want to marry one of these self-sufficient independent, professional women, of course."

"I do hope, Viva," said her mother, "that you're not letting that Dr. Bellair put foolish ideas into your head."

"I want to do something to support myself—sometime, Mother. I can't live on my parents forever."

"You be patient, child. There's money enough for you to live on. It's a woman's place to wait," put in Mr. Lane.

"How long?" inquired Vivian. "I'm twenty-five. No man has asked me to marry him yet. Some of the women in this town have waited thirty—forty—fifty—sixty years. No one has asked them."

"I was married at sixteen," suddenly remarked Vivian's grandmother. "And my mother wasn't but fifteen. Huh!" A sudden little derisive noise she made; such as used to be written "humph!"

For the past five years, Mrs. Pettigrew had made her home with the Lanes. Mrs. Lane herself was but a feeble replica of her energetic parent. There was but seventeen years difference in their ages, and comparative idleness with some ill-health on the part of the daughter, had made the difference appear less.

Mrs. Pettigrew had but a poor opinion of the present generation. In her active youth she had reared a large family on a small income; in her active middle-age, she had trotted about from daughter's house to son's house, helping with the grandchildren. And now she still trotted about in all weathers, visiting among the neighbors and vibrating as regularly as a pendulum between her daughter's house and the public library.

The books she brought home were mainly novels, and if she perused anything else in the severe quiet of the reading-room, she did not talk about it. Indeed, it was a striking characteristic of Mrs. Pettigrew that she talked very little, though she listened to all that went on with a bright and beady eye, as of a highly intelligent parrot. And now, having dropped her single remark into the conversation, she shut her lips tight as was her habit, and drew another ball of worsted from the black bag that always hung at her elbow.

She was making one of those perennial knitted garments, which, in her young days, were called "Cardigan jackets," later "Jerseys," and now by the offensive name of "sweater." These she constructed in great numbers, and their probable expense was a source of discussion in the town. "How do you find friends enough to give them to?" they asked her, and she would smile enigmatically and reply, "Good presents make good friends."

"If a woman minds her P's and Q's she can get a husband easy enough," insisted the invalid. "Just shove that lamp nearer, Vivian, will you."

Vivian moved the lamp. Her mother moved her chair to follow it and dropped her darning egg, which the girl handed to her.

"Supper's ready," announced a hard-featured middle-aged woman, opening the dining-room door.

At this moment the gate clicked, and a firm step was heard coming up the path.

"Gracious, that's the minister!" cried Mrs. Lane. "He said he'd be in this afternoon if he got time. I thought likely 'twould be to supper."

She received him cordially, and insisted on his staying, slipping out presently to open a jar of quinces.

The Reverend Otis Williams was by no means loathe to take

occasional meals with his parishioners. It was noted that, in making pastoral calls, he began with the poorer members of his flock, and frequently arrived about meal-time at the houses of those whose cooking he approved.

"It is always a treat to take supper here," he said. "Not feeling well, Mr. Lane? I'm sorry to hear it. Ah! Mrs. Pettigrew! Is that jacket for me, by any chance? A little sombre, isn't it? Good evening, Vivian. You are looking well—as you always do."

Vivian did not like him. He had married her mother, he had christened her, she had "sat under" him for long, dull, uninterrupted years; yet still she didn't like him.

"A chilly evening, Mr. Lane," he pursued.

"That's what I say," his host agreed. "Vivian says it isn't; I say it is."

"Disagreement in the family! This won't do Vivian," said the minister jocosely. "Duty to parents, you know! Duty to parents!"

"Does duty to parents alter the temperature?" the girl asked, in a voice of quiet sweetness, yet with a rebellious spark in her soft eyes.

"Huh!" said her grandmother—and dropped her gray ball. Vivian picked it up and the old lady surreptitiously patted her.

"Pardon me," said the reverend gentleman to Mrs. Pettigrew, "did you speak?"

"No," said the old lady, "Seldom do."

"Silence is golden, Mrs. Pettigrew. Silence is golden. Speech is silver, but silence is golden. It is a rare gift."

Mrs. Pettigrew set her lips so tightly that they quite disappeared, leaving only a thin dented line in her smoothly pale face. She was called by the neighbors "wonderfully well preserved," a phrase she herself despised. Some visitor, new to the town, had the hardihood to use it to her face once. "Huh!" was the response. "I'm just sixty. Henry Haskins and George Baker and Stephen Doolittle are all older'n I am—and still doing business, doing it better'n any of the young folks as far as I can see. You don't compare them to canned pears, do you?"

Mr. Williams knew her value in church work, and took no umbrage at her somewhat inimical expression; particularly as just then Mrs. Lane appeared and asked them to walk out to supper.

Vivian sat among them, restrained and courteous, but inwardly at war with her surroundings. Here was her mother, busy, responsible, serving creamed codfish and hot biscuit; her father, eating wheezily, and finding fault with the biscuit, also with the codfish; her grandmother, bright-eyed, thin-lipped and silent. Vivian got on well with her grandmother, though neither of them talked much.

"My mother used to say that the perfect supper was cake, preserves, hot bread, and a 'relish,'" said Mr. Williams genially. "You have the perfect supper, Mrs. Lane."

"I'm glad if you enjoy it, I'm sure," said that lady. "I'm fond of a bit of salt myself."

"And what are you reading now, Vivian," he asked paternally.

"Ward," she answered, modestly and briefly.

"Ward? Dr. Ward of the *Centurion?*"

Vivian smiled her gentlest.

"Oh, no," she replied; "Lester F. Ward, the Sociologist."

"Poor stuff, I think!" said her father. "Girls have no business to read such things."

"I wish you'd speak to Vivian about it, Mr. Williams. She's got beyond me," protested her mother.

"Huh!" said Mrs. Pettigrew. "I'd like some more of that quince, Laura."

"My dear young lady, you are not reading books of which your parents disapprove, I hope?" urged the minister.

"Shouldn't I—ever?" asked the girl, in her soft, disarming manner. "I'm surely old enough!"

"The duty of a daughter is not measured by years," he replied sonorously. "Does parental duty cease? Are you not yet a child in your father's house?"

"Is a daughter always a child if she lives at home?" inquired the girl, as one seeking instruction.

He set down his cup and wiped his lips, flushing somewhat.

"The duty of a daughter begins at the age when she can understand the distinction between right and wrong," he said, "and continues as long as she is blessed with parents."

"And what is it?" she asked, large-eyed, attentive.

"What is it?" he repeated, looking at her in some surprise. "It is submission, obedience—obedience."

"I see. So Mother ought to obey Grandmother," she pursued meditatively, and Mrs. Pettigrew nearly choked in her tea.

Vivian was boiling with rebellion. To sit there and be lectured at the table, to have her father complain of her, her mother invite pastoral interference, the minister preach like that. She slapped her grandmother's shoulder, readjusted the little knit shawl on the straight back—and refrained from further speech.

When Mrs. Pettigrew could talk, she demanded suddenly of the minister, "Have you read Campbell's New Theology?" and from that on they were all occupied in listening to Mr. Williams' strong, clear and extensive views on the subject—which lasted into the parlor again.

Vivian sat for awhile in the chair nearest the window, where some thin thread of air might possibly leak in, and watched the minister with a curious expression. All her life he had been held up to her as a person to honor, as a man of irreproachable character, great learning and wisdom. Of late she found with a sense of surprise that she did not honor him at all. He seemed to her suddenly like a relic of past ages, a piece of an old parchment—or papyrus. In the light of the studies she had been pursuing in the well-stored town library, the teachings of this worthy old gentleman appeared a jumble of age-old traditions, superimposed one upon another.

"He's a palimpsest," she said to herself, "and a poor palimpsest at that."

She sat with her shapely hands quiet in her lap while her grandmother's shining needles twinkled in the dark wool, and her mother's slim crochet hook ran along the widening spaces of some thin, white, fuzzy thing. The rich powers of her young womanhood longed for occupation, but she could never hypnotize herself with "fancy-work." Her work must be worth while. She felt the crushing cramp and loneliness of a young mind, really stronger than those about her, yet held in dumb subjection. She could not solace herself by loving them; her father would have none of it, and her mother had small use for what she called "sentiment." All her life Vivian had longed for more loving, both to give and take; but no one ever imagined it of her, she was so quiet and repressed in manner. The local opinion was that if a woman had a head, she could not have a heart; and as to having a body—it was indelicate to consider such a thing.

"I mean to have six children," Vivian had planned when she was younger. "And they shall never be hungry for more loving." She meant to make up to her vaguely imagined future family for all that her own youth missed.

Even Grandma, though far more sympathetic in temperament, was not given to demonstration, and Vivian solaced her big, tender heart by cuddling all the babies she could reach, and petting cats and dogs when no children were to be found.

Presently she arose and bade a courteous good night to the still prolix parson.

"I'm going over to Sue's," she said, and went out.

THERE WAS A moon again—a low, large moon, hazily brilliant. The air was sweet with the odors of scarce-gone Summer, of coming Autumn.

The girl stood still, half-way down the path, and looked steadily into that silver radiance. Moonlight always filled her heart with a vague excitement, a feeling that something ought to happen—soon.

This flat, narrow life, so long, so endlessly long—would nothing ever end it? Nine years since Morton went away! Nine years since the strange, invading thrill of her first kiss! Back of that was only childhood; these years really constituted Life; and Life, in the girl's eyes, was a dreary treadmill.

She was externally quiet, and by conscience dutiful; so dutiful, so quiet, so without powers of expression, that the ache of an unsatisfied heart, the stir of young ambitions, were wholly unsuspected by those about her. A studious, earnest, thoughtful girl—but study alone does not supply life's needs, nor does such friendship as her life afforded.

Susie was "a dear"—Susie was Morton's sister, and she was very fond of her. But that bright-haired child did not understand—could not understand—all that she needed.

Then came Mrs. St. Cloud into her life, stirring the depths of romance, of the buried past, and of the unborn future. From her she learned to face a life of utter renunciation, to be true, true to her ideals, true to her principles, true to the past, to be patient; and to wait.

So strengthened, she had turned a deaf ear to such possible voice of admiration as might have come from the scant membership of the Young Men's Bible Class, leaving them the more devoted to Scripture study. There was no thin ring to turn upon her finger; but, for lack of better token, she had saved the rose she wore upon her breast that night, keeping it hidden among her precious things.

And then, into the gray, flat current of her daily life, sharply across the trend of Mrs. St. Cloud's soft influence, had come a new force—Dr. Bellair.

Vivian liked her, yet felt afraid, a slight, shivering hesitancy as before a too cold bath, a subtle sense that this breezy woman, strong, cheerful, full of new ideas, if not ideals, and radiating actual power, power used and enjoyed, might in some way change the movement of her life.

Change she desired, she longed for, but dreaded the unknown.

Slowly she followed the long garden path, paused lingeringly by that rough garden seat, went through and closed the gate.

3

THE OUTBREAK

There comes a time
After white months of ice—
Slow months of ice—long months of ice—
There comes a time when the still floods below
Rise, lift, and overflow—
Fast, far they go.

Miss Orella sat in her low armless rocker, lifting perplexed, patient eyes to look up at Dr. Bellair.

Dr. Bellair stood squarely before her, stood easily, on broad-soled, low-heeled shoes, and looked down at Miss Orella; her eyes were earnest, compelling, full of hope and cheer.

"You are as pretty as a girl, Orella," she observed irrelevantly.

Miss Orella blushed. She was not used to compliments, even from a woman, and did not know how to take them.

"How you talk!" she murmured shyly.

"I mean to talk," continued the doctor, "until you listen to reason."

Reason in this case, to Dr. Bellair's mind, lay in her advice to Miss Elder to come West with her—to live.

"I don't see how I can. It's—it's such a Complete Change."

Miss Orella spoke as if Change were equivalent to Sin, or at least to Danger.

"Do you good. As a physician, I can prescribe nothing better. You need a complete change if anybody ever did."

"Why, Jane! I am quite well."

"I didn't say you were sick. But you are in an advanced stage of *arthritis deformans* of the soul. The whole town's got it!"

The doctor tramped up and down the little room, freeing her mind.

"I never saw such bed-ridden intellects in my life! I suppose it was so when I was a child—and I was too young to notice it. But surely it's worse now. The world goes faster and faster every day, the people who keep still get farther behind! I'm fond of you, Rella. You've got an intellect, and a conscience, and a will—a will like iron. But you spend most of your strength in keeping yourself down. Now, do wake up and use it to break loose! You don't have to stay here. Come out to Colorado with me—and Grow."

Miss Elder moved uneasily in her chair. She laid her small embroidery hoop on the table, and straightened out the loose threads of silk, the doctor watching her impatiently.

"I'm too old," she said at length.

Jane Bellair laughed aloud, shortly.

"Old!" she cried. "You're five years younger than I am. You're only thirty-six! Old! Why, child, your life's before you—to make."

"You don't realize, Jane. You struck out for yourself so young—and you've grown up out there—it seems to be so different—there."

"It is. People aren't afraid to move. What have you got here you so hate to leave, Rella?"

"Why, it's—Home."

"Yes. It's home—now. Are you happy in it?"

"I'm—contented."

"Don't you deceive yourself, Rella. You are not contented—not by a long chalk. You are doing your duty as you see it; and you've kept yourself down so long you've almost lost the power of motion. I'm trying to galvanize you awake—and I mean to do it."

"You might as well sit down while you're doing it, anyway," Miss Elder suggested meekly.

Dr. Bellair sat down, selecting a formidable fiddle-backed chair, the unflinching determination of its widely-placed feet being repeated by her own square toes. She placed herself in front of her friend and leaned forward, elbows on knees, her strong, intelligent hands clasped loosely.

"What have you got to look forward to, Rella?"

"I want to see Susie happily married—"

"I said *you*—not Susie."

"Oh—me? Why, I hope some day Morton will come back—"

"I said *you*—not Morton."

"Why I—you know I have friends, Jane—and neighbors. And some day, perhaps—I mean to go abroad."

"Are you scolding Aunt Rella again, Dr. Bellair. I won't stand it." Pretty Susie stood in the door smiling.

"Come and help me then," the doctor said, "and it won't sound so much like scolding."

"I want Mort's letter—to show to Viva," the girl answered, and slipped out with it.

She sat with Vivian on the stiff little sofa in the back room; the arms of the two girls were around one another, and they read the letter together. More than six months had passed since his last one.

It was not much of a letter. Vivian took it in her own hands and went through it again, carefully. The "Remember me to Viva—unless she's married," at the end did not seem at all satisfying. Still it might mean more than appeared—far more. Men were reticent and proud, she had read. It was perfectly possible that he might be concealing deep emotion under the open friendliness. He was in no condition to speak freely, to come back and claim her. He did not wish her to feel bound to him. She had discussed it with Mrs. St. Cloud, shrinkingly, tenderly, led on by tactful, delicate, questions, by the longing of her longing heart for expression and sympathy.

"A man who cannot marry must not speak of marriage—it is not honorable," her friend had told her.

"Couldn't he—write to me—as a friend?"

And the low-voiced lady had explained with a little sigh that men thought little of friendship with women. "I have tried, all my life, to be a true and helpful friend to men, to such men as seemed worthy, and they so often—misunderstood."

The girl, sympathetic and admiring, thought hotly of how other people misunderstood this noble, lovely soul; how they even hinted that she "tried to attract men," a deadly charge in Bainville.

"No," Mrs. St. Cloud had told her, "he might love you better than all the world—yet not write to you—till he was ready to say 'come.' And, of course, he wouldn't say anything in his letters to his aunt."

So Vivian sat there, silent, weaving frail dreams out of "remember me to Viva—unless she's married." That last clause might mean much.

Dr. Bellair's voice sounded clear and insistent in the next room.

"She's trying to persuade Aunt Rella to go West!" said Susie. "Wouldn't it be funny if she did!"

In Susie's eyes her Aunt's age was as the age of mountains, and also her fixity. Since she could remember, Aunt Rella, always palely pretty and neat, like the delicate, faintly-colored Spring flowers of New England, had presided over the small white house, the small green garden and the large black and white school-room. In her vacation she sewed, keeping that quiet wardrobe of hers in exquisite order—and also making Susie's pretty dresses. To think of Aunt Orella actually "breaking up housekeeping," giving up her school, leaving Bainville, was like a vision of trees walking.

To Dr. Jane Bellair, forty-one, vigorous, successful, full of new plans and purposes, Miss Elder's life appeared as an arrested girlhood, stagnating unnecessarily in this quiet town, while all the world was open to her.

"I couldn't think of leaving Susie!" protested Miss Orella.

"Bring her along," said the doctor. "Best thing in the world for her!"

She rose and came to the door. The two girls made a pretty picture. Vivian's oval face, with its smooth Madonna curves under the encircling wreath of soft, dark plaits, and the long grace of her figure, delicately built, yet strong, beside the pink, plump little Susie, roguish and pretty, with the look that made everyone want to take care of her.

"Come in here, girls," said the doctor. "I want you to help me. You're young enough to be movable, I hope."

They cheerfully joined the controversy, but Miss Orella found small support in them.

"Why don't you do it, Auntie!" Susie thought it an excellent joke. "I suppose you could teach school in Denver as well as here. And you could Vote! Oh, Auntie—to think of your Voting!"

Miss Elder, too modestly feminine, too inherently conservative even to be an outspoken "Anti," fairly blushed at the idea.

"She's hesitating on your account," Dr. Bellair explained to the girl. "Wants to see you safely married! I tell her you'll have a thousandfold better opportunities in Colorado than you ever will here."

Vivian was grieved. She had heard enough of this getting married, and had expected Dr. Bellair to hold a different position.

"Surely, that's not the only thing to do," she protested.

"No, but it's a very important thing to do—and to do right. It's a woman's duty."

Vivian groaned in spirit. That again!

The doctor watched her understandingly.

"If women only did their duty in that line there wouldn't be so much unhappiness in the world," she said. "All you New England girls sit here and cut one another's throats. You can't possible marry, your boys go West, you overcrowd the labor market, lower wages, steadily drive the weakest sisters down till they—drop."

They heard the back door latch lift and close again, a quick, decided step—and Mrs. Pettigrew joined them.

Miss Elder greeted her cordially, and the old lady seated herself in the halo of the big lamp, as one well accustomed to the chair.

"Go right on," she said—and knitted briskly.

"Do take my side, Mrs. Pettigrew," Miss Orella implored her. "Jane Bellair is trying to pull me up by the roots and transplant me to Colorado."

"And she says I shall have a better chance to marry out there—and ought to do it!" said Susie, very solemnly. "And Vivian objects to being shown the path of duty."

Vivian smiled. Her quiet, rather sad face lit with sudden sparkling beauty when she smiled.

"Grandma knows I hate that—point of view," she said. "I think men and women ought to be friends, and not always be thinking about—that."

"I have some real good friends—boys, I mean," Susie agreed, looking so serious in her platonic boast that even Vivian was a little amused, and Dr. Bellair laughed outright.

"You won't have a 'friend' in that sense till you're fifty, Miss Susan—if you ever do. There can be, there are, real friendships between men and women, but most of that talk is—talk, sometimes worse.

"I knew a woman once, ever so long ago," the doctor continued musingly, clasping her hands behind her head, "a long way from here—in a college town—who talked about 'friends.' She was married. She was a 'good' woman—perfectly 'good' woman. Her husband was not a very good man, I've heard, and strangely impatient of her virtues. She had a string of boys—college boys—always at her heels. Quite too young and too charming she was for this friendship game. She said that such a friendship was 'an ennobling influence' for the boys. She called them her 'acolytes.' Lots of them were fairly mad about her—one young chap was so desperate over it that he shot himself."

There was a pained silence.

"I don't see what this has to do with going to Colorado," said Mrs. Pettigrew, looking from one to the other with a keen, observing eye. "What's your plan, Dr. Bellair?"

"Why, I'm trying to persuade my old friend here to leave this place, change her occupation, come out to Colorado with me, and grow up. She's a case of arrested development."

"She wants me to keep boarders!" Miss Elder plaintively protested to Mrs. Pettigrew.

That lady was not impressed.

"It's quite a different matter out there, Mrs. Pettigrew," the doctor explained. " 'Keeping boarders' in this country goes to the tune of 'Come Ye Disconsolate!' It's a doubtful refuge for women who are widows or would be better off if they were. Where I live it's a sure thing if well managed—it's a good business."

Mrs. Pettigrew wore an unconvinced aspect.

"What do you call 'a good business?' " she asked.

"The house I have in mind cleared a thousand a year when it was in right hands. That's not bad, over and above one's board and lodging. That house is in the market now. I've just had a letter from a friend about it. Orella could go out with me, and step right into Mrs. Annerly's shoes—she's just giving up."

"What'd she give up for?" Mrs. Pettigrew inquired suspiciously.

"Oh—she got married; they all do. There are three men to one woman in that town, you see."

"I didn't know there was such a place in the world—unless it was a man-of-war," remarked Susie, looking much interested.

Dr. Bellair went on more quietly.

"It's not even a risk, Mrs. Pettigrew. Rella has a cousin who would gladly run this house for her. She's admitted that much. So there's no loss here, and she's got her home to come back to. I can write to Dick Hale to nail the proposition at once. She can go when I go, in about a fortnight, and I'll guarantee the first year definitely."

"I wouldn't think of letting you do that, Jane! And if it's as good as you say, there's no need. But a fortnight! To leave home—in a fortnight!"

"What are the difficulties?" the old lady inquired. "There are always some difficulties."

"You are right, there," agreed the doctor. "The difficulties in this place are servants. But just now there's a special chance in that line. Dick says the best cook in town is going begging. I'll read you his letter."

She produced it, promptly, from the breast pocket of her neat coat. Dr. Bellair wore rather short, tailored skirts of first-class material; natty, starched blouses—silk ones for "dress," and perfectly fitting light coats. Their color and texture might vary with the season, but their pockets, never.

" 'My dear Jane' (This is my best friend out there—a doctor, too. We were in the same class, both college and medical school. We fight—he's a misogynist of the worst type—but we're good friends all the same.) 'Why don't you come back? My boys are lonesome without you, and I am overworked—you left so many mishandled invalids for me to struggle with. Your boarding house is going to the dogs. Mrs. Annerly got worse and worse, failed completely and has cleared out, with a species of husband, I believe. The owner has put in a sort of caretaker, and the roomers get board outside—it's better than what they were having. Moreover, the best cook in town is hunting a job. Wire me and I'll nail her. You know the place pays well. Now, why don't you give up your unnatural attempt to be a doctor and assume woman's proper sphere? Come back and keep house!' "

"He's a great tease, but he tells the truth. The house is there, crying to be kept. The boarders are there—unfed. Now, Orella Elder, why don't you wake up and seize the opportunity?"

Miss Orella was thinking.

"Where's that last letter of Morton's?"

Susie looked for it. Vivian handed it to her, and Miss Elder read it once more.

"There's plenty of homeless boys out there besides yours, Orella," the doctor assured her. "Come on—and bring both these girls with you. It's a chance for any girl, Miss Lane."

But her friend did not hear her. She found what she was looking for in the letter and read it aloud. "I'm on the road again now, likely to be doing Colorado most of the year if things go right. It's a fine country."

Susie hopped up with a little cry.

"Just the thing, Aunt Rella! Let's go out and surprise Mort. He thinks we are just built into the ground here. Won't it be fun, Viva?"

Vivian had risen from her seat and stood at the window, gazing out with unseeing eyes at the shadowy little front yard. Morton might be there. She might see him. But—was it womanly to go there—for that? There were other reasons, surely. She had longed for freedom, for a chance to grow, to do something in life—something great and beautiful! Perhaps this was the opening of the gate, the opportunity of a lifetime.

"You folks are so strong on duty," the doctor was saying, "Why can't you see a real duty in this? I tell you, the place is full of men that need mothering, and sistering—good honest sweethearting and marrying, too. Come on, Rella. Do bigger work than you've ever done yet—and, as I said, bring both these nice girls with you. What do you say, Miss Lane?"

Vivian turned to her, her fine face flushed with hope, yet with a small Greek fret on the broad forehead.

"I'd like to, very much, Dr. Bellair—on some accounts. But—" She could not quite voice her dim objections, her obscure withdrawals; and so fell back on the excuse of childhood—"I'm sure Mother wouldn't let me."

Dr. Bellair smiled broadly.

"Aren't you over twenty-one?" she asked.

"I'm twenty-five," the girl replied, with proud acceptance of a life long done—as one who owned to ninety-seven.

"And self-supporting?" pursued the doctor.

Vivian flushed.

"No—not yet," she answered; "but I mean to be."

"Exactly! Now's your chance. Break away now, my dear, and come West. You can get work—start a kindergarten, or something. I know you love children."

The girl's heart rose within her in a great throb of hope.

"Oh—if I *could!*" she exclaimed, and even as she said it, rose half-conscious memories of the low, sweet tones of Mrs. St. Cloud. "It is a woman's place to wait—and to endure."

She heard a step on the walk outside—looked out.

"Why, here is Mrs. St. Cloud!" she cried.

"Guess I'll clear out," said the doctor, as Susie ran to the door. She was shy, socially.

"Nonsense, Jane," said her hostess, whispering. "Mrs. St. Cloud is no stranger. She's Mrs. Williams' sister—been here for years."

She came in at the word, her head and shoulders wreathed in a pearl gray shining veil, her soft long robe held up.

"I saw your light, Miss Elder, and thought I'd stop in for a moment. Good evening, Mrs. Pettigrew—and Miss Susie. Ah! Vivian!"

"This is my friend, Dr. Bellair—Mrs. St. Cloud," Miss Elder was saying. But Dr. Bellair bowed a little stiffly, not coming forward.

"I've met Mrs. St. Cloud before, I think—when she was 'Mrs. James.' "

The lady's face grew sad.

"Ah, you knew my first husband! I lost him—many years ago—typhoid fever."

"I think I heard," said the doctor. And then, feeling that some expression of sympathy was called for, she added, "Too bad."

Not all Miss Elder's gentle hospitality, Mrs. Pettigrew's bright-eyed interest, Susie's efforts at polite attention, and Vivian's visible sympathy could compensate Mrs. St. Cloud for one inimical presence.

"You must have been a mere girl in those days," she said sweetly. "What a lovely little town it was—under the big trees."

"It certainly was," the doctor answered dryly.

"There is such a fine atmosphere in a college town, I think," pursued the lady. "Especially in a co-educational town—don't you think so?"

Vivian was a little surprised. She had had an idea that her admired friend did not approve of co-education. She must have been mistaken.

"Such a world of old memories as you call up, Dr. Bellair," their visitor pursued. "Those quiet, fruitful days! You remember Dr. Black's lectures? Of course you do, better than I. What a fine man he was! And the beautiful music club we had one Winter—and my little private dancing class—do you remember that? Such nice boys, Miss Elder! I used to call them my acolytes."

Susie gave a little gulp, and coughed to cover it.

"I guess you'll have to excuse me, ladies," said Dr. Bellair. "Good-night." And she walked upstairs.

Vivian's face flushed and paled and flushed again. A cold pain was trying to enter her heart, and she was trying to keep it out. Her grandmother glanced sharply from one face to the other.

"Glad to've met you, Mrs. St. Cloud," she said, bobbing up with decision. "Good-night, Rella—and Susie. Come on child. It's a wonder your mother hasn't sent after us."

For once Vivian was glad to go.

"That's a good scheme of Jane Bellair's, don't you think so?" asked the old lady as they shut the gate behind them.

"I—why yes—I don't see why not."

Vivian was still dizzy with the blow to her heart's idol. All the soft, still dream-world she had so labored to keep pure and beautiful seemed to shake and waver swimmingly. She could not return to it. The flat white face of her home loomed before her, square, hard, hideously unsympathetic—

"Grandma," said she, stopping that lady suddenly and laying a pleading hand on her arm, "Grandma, I believe I'll go."

Mrs. Pettigrew nodded decisively.

"I thought you would," she said.

"Do you blame me, Grandma?"

"Not a mite, child. Not a mite. But I'd sleep on it, if I were you."

And Vivian slept on it—so far as she slept at all.

4

TRANSPLANTED

Sometimes a plant in its own habitat
Is overcrowded, starved, oppressed and daunted;
A palely feeble thing; yet rises quickly,
Growing in height and vigor, blooming thickly,
When far transplanted.

The days between Vivian's decision and her departure were harder than she had foreseen. It took some courage to make the choice. Had she been alone, independent, quite free to change, the move would have been difficult enough; but to make her plan and hold to it in the face of a disapproving town, and the definite opposition of her parents, was a heavy undertaking.

By habit she would have turned to Mrs. St. Cloud for advice; but between her and that lady now rose the vague image of a young boy, dead,—she could never feel the same to her again.

Dr. Bellair proved a tower of strength. "My dear girl," she would say to her, patiently, but with repressed intensity, "do remember that you are *not* a child! You are twenty-five years old. You are a grown woman, and have as much right to decide for yourself as a grown man. This isn't wicked—it is a wise move; a practical one. Do you want to grow up like the rest of the useless single women in this little social cemetery?"

Her mother took it very hard. "I don't see how you can think of leaving us. We're getting old now—and here's Grandma to take care of—"

"Huh!" said that lady, with such marked emphasis that Mrs. Lane hastily changed the phrase to "I mean to *be with*—you do like to have Vivian with you, you can't deny that, Mother."

"But Mama," said the girl, "you are not old; you are only forty-three. I am sorry to leave you—I am really; but it isn't forever! I can come back. And you don't really need me. Sarah runs the house exactly as you like; you don't depend on me for a thing, and never did. As to Grandma!"—and she looked affectionately at the old lady—"she don't need me nor anybody else. She's independent if ever anybody was. She won't miss me a mite—will you Grandma?"

Mrs. Pettigrew looked at her for a moment, the corners of her mouth tucked in tightly. "No," she said, "I shan't miss you a mite!"

Vivian was a little grieved at the prompt acquiescence. She felt nearer to her grandmother in many ways than to either parent. "Well, I'll miss you!" said she, going to her and kissing her smooth pale cheek, "I'll miss you awfully!"

Mr. Lane expressed his disapproval most thoroughly, and more than once; then retired into gloomy silence, alternated with violent dissuasion; but since a woman of twenty-five is certainly free to choose her way of life, and there was no real objection to this change, except that it *was* a change, and therefore dreaded, his opposition, though unpleasant, was not prohibitive. Vivian's independent fortune of $87.50, the savings of many years, made the step possible, even without his assistance.

There were two weeks of exceeding disagreeableness in the household, but Vivian kept her temper and her determination under a rain of tears, a hail of criticism, and heavy wind of argument and exhortation. All her friends and neighbors, and many who were neither, joined in the effort to dissuade her; but she stood firm as the martyrs of old.

Heredity plays strange tricks with us. Somewhere under the girl's dumb gentleness and patience lay a store of quiet strength from some Pilgrim Father or Mother. Never before had she set her will against her parents; conscience had always told her to submit. Now conscience told her to rebel, and she did. She made her personal arrangements, said goodbye to her friends, declined to discuss with anyone, was sweet and quiet and kind at home, and finally appeared at the appointed hour on the platform of the little station.

Numbers of curious neighbors were there to see them off, all who knew them and could spare the time seemed to be on hand. Vivian's mother came, but her father did not.

At the last moment, just as the train drew in, Grandma appeared, serene and brisk, descending, with an impressive amount of hand baggage, from "the hack."

"Goodbye, Laura," she said. "I think these girls need a chaperon. I'm going too."

So blasting was the astonishment caused by this proclamation, and so short a time remained to express it, that they presently found themselves gliding off in the big Pullman, all staring at one another in silent amazement.

"I hate discussion," said Mrs. Pettigrew.

NONE OF THESE LADIES were used to traveling, save Dr. Bellair, who had made the cross continent trip often enough to think nothing of it.

The unaccustomed travelers found much excitement in the journey. As women, embarking on a new, and, in the eyes of their friends, highly doubtful enterprise, they had emotion to spare; and to be confronted at the outset by a totally unexpected grandmother was too much for immediate comprehension.

She looked from one to the other, sparkling, triumphant.

"I made up my mind, same as you did, hearing Jane Bellair talk," she explained. "Sounded like good sense. I always wanted to travel, always, and never had the opportunity. This was a real good chance." Her mouth shut, tightened, widened, drew into a crinkly delighted smile.

They sat still staring at her.

"You needn't look at me like that! I guess it's a free country! I bought my ticket—sent for it same as you did. And I didn't have to ask *anybody*—I'm no daughter. My duty, as far as I know it, is *done!* This is a pleasure trip!"

She was triumph incarnate.

"And you never said a word!" This from Vivian.

"Not a word. Saved lots of trouble. Take care of me indeed! Laura needn't think I'm dependent on her *yet!*"

Vivian's heart rather yearned over her mother, thus doubly bereft.

"The truth is," her grandmother went on, "Samuel wants to go to Florida the worst way; I heard 'em talking about it! He wasn't willing to go alone—not he! Wants somebody to hear him cough, *I* say! And Laura couldn't go—'Mother was so dependent'—*Huh!*"

Vivian began to smile. She knew this had been talked over, and given up on that account. She herself could have been easily disposed of, but Mrs. Lane chose to think her mother a lifelong charge.

"Act as if I was ninety!" the old lady burst forth again. "I'll show 'em!"

"I think you're dead right, Mrs. Pettigrew," said Dr. Bellair. "Sixty isn't anything. You ought to have twenty years of enjoyable life yet, before they call you 'old'—maybe more."

Mrs. Pettigrew cocked an eye at her. "My grandmother lived to be a hundred and four," said she, "and kept on working up to the last year. I don't know about enjoyin' life, but she was useful for pretty near a solid century. After she broke her hip the last time she sat still and sewed and knitted. After her eyes gave out she took to hooking rugs."

"I hope it will be forty years, Mrs. Pettigrew," said Sue, "and I'm real glad you're coming. It'll make it more like home."

Miss Elder was a little slow in accommodating herself to this new accession. She liked Mrs. Pettigrew very much—but—a grandmother thus airily at large seemed to unsettle the foundations of things. She was polite, even cordial, but evidently found it difficult to accept the facts.

"Besides," said Mrs. Pettigrew, "you may not get all those boarders at once and I'll be one to count on. I stopped at the bank this morning and had 'em arrange for my account out in Carston. They were some surprised, but there was no time to ask questions!" She relapsed into silence and gazed with keen interest at the whirling landscape.

Throughout the journey she proved the best of travelers; was never car-sick, slept well in the joggling berth, enjoyed the food, and continually astonished them by producing from her handbag the most diverse and unlooked for conveniences. An old-fashioned traveller had forgotten her watchkey—Grandma produced an automatic one warranted to fit anything. "Takes up mighty little room—and I thought maybe it would come in handy," she said.

She had a small bottle of liquid courtplaster, and plenty of the solid kind. She had a delectable lotion for the hands, a real treasure on the dusty journey; also a tiny corkscrew, a strong pair of "pinchers," sewing materials, playing cards, string, safety-pins, elastic bands, lime drops, stamped envelopes, smelling salts, troches, needles and thread.

"Did you bring a trunk, Grandma?" asked Vivian.

"Two," said Grandma, "excess baggage. All paid for and checked."

"How did you ever learn to arrange things so well?" Sue asked admiringly.

"Read about it," the old lady answered. "There's no end of directions nowadays. I've been studying up."

She was so gleeful and triumphant, so variously useful, so steadily gay and stimulating, that they all grew to value her presence long before they reached Carston; but they had no conception of the ultimate effect of a resident grandmother in that new and bustling town.

To Vivian the journey was a daily and nightly revelation. She had read much but traveled very little, never at night. The spreading beauty of the land was to her a new stimulus; she watched by the hour the endless panorama fly past her window, its countless shades of green, the brown and red soil, the fleeting dashes of color where wild flowers gathered thickly. She was repeatedly impressed by seeing suddenly beside her the name of some town which had only existed in her mind as "capital city" associated with "principal exports" and "bounded on the north."

At night, sleeping little, she would raise her curtain and look out, sideways, at the stars. Big shadowy trees ran by, steep cuttings rose like a wall of darkness, and the hilly curves of open country rose and fell against the sky line like a shaken carpet.

She faced the long, bright vistas of the car and studied people's faces—such different people from any she had seen before. A heavy young man with small, light eyes, sat near by, and cast frequent glances at both the girls, going by their seat at intervals. Vivian considered this distinctly rude, and Sue did not like his looks, so he got nothing for his pains, yet even this added color to the day.

The strange, new sense of freedom grew in her heart, a feeling of lightness and hope and unfolding purpose.

There was continued discussion as to what the girls should do.

"We can be waitresses for Auntie till we get something else," Sue practically insisted. "The doctor says it will be hard to get good service and I'm sure the boarders would like us."

"You can both find work if you want it. What do you want to do, Vivian?" asked Dr. Bellair, not for the first time.

Vivian was still uncertain.

"I love children best," she said. "I could teach—but I haven't a certificate. I'd *love* a kindergarten; I've studied that—at home."

"Shouldn't wonder if you could get up a kindergarten right off," the doctor assured her. "Meantime, as this kitten says, you could help Miss Elder out and turn an honest penny while you're waiting."

"Wouldn't it—interfere with my teaching later?" the girl inquired.

"Not a bit, not a bit. We're not so foolish out here. We'll fix you up all right in no time."

It was morning when they arrived at last and came out of the cindery, noisy crowded cars into the wide, clean, brilliant stillness of the high plateau. They drew deep breaths; the doctor squared her shoulders with a glad, homecoming smile. Vivian lifted her head and faced the new surroundings as an unknown world. Grandma gazed all ways, still cheerful, and their baggage accrued about them as a rampart.

A big bearded man, carelessly dressed, whirled up in a dusty runabout, and stepped out smiling. He seized Dr. Bellair by both hands, and shook them warmly.

"Thought I'd catch you, Johnny," he said. "Glad to see you back. If you've got the landlady, I've got the cook!"

"Here we are," said she. "Miss Orella Elder—Dr. Hale; Mrs. Pettigrew, Miss Susie Elder, Miss Lane—Dr. Richard Hale."

He bowed deeply to Mrs. Pettigrew, shook hands with Miss Orella, and addressed himself to her, giving only a cold nod to the two girls, and quite turning away from them.

Susie, in quiet aside to Vivian, made unfavorable comment.

"This is your Western chivalry, is it?" she said. "Even Bainville does better than that."

"I don't know why we should mind," Vivian answered. "It's Dr. Bellair's friend; he don't care anything about us."

But she was rather of Sue's opinion.

The big man took Dr. Bellair in his car, and they followed in a station carriage, eagerly observing their new surroundings, and surprised, as most Easterners are, by the broad beauty of the streets and the modern conveniences everywhere—electric cars, electric lights, telephones, soda fountains, where they had rather expected to find tents and wigwams.

The house, when they were all safely within it, turned out to be "just like a real house," as Sue said; and proved even more attractive than the doctor had described it. It was a big, rambling thing, at home they would have called it a hotel, with its neat little sign, "The Cottonwoods," and Vivian finally concluded that it looked like a seaside boarding house, built for the purpose.

A broad piazza ran all across the front, the door opening into a big square hall, a sort of general sitting-room; on either side were four good rooms, opening on a transverse passage. The long dining-room and kitchen were in the rear of the hall.

Dr. Bellair had two, her office fronting on the side street, with a bedroom behind it. They gave Mrs. Pettigrew the front corner room on that side and kept the one opening from the hall as their own parlor. In the opposite wing was Miss Elder's room next the hall, and the girls in the outer back corner, while the two front ones on that side were kept for the most impressive and high-priced boarders.

Mrs. Pettigrew regarded her apartments with suspicion as being too "easy."

"I don't mind stairs," she said. "Dr. Bellair has to be next her office—but why do I have to be next Dr. Bellair?"

It was represented to her that she would be nearer to everything that went on and she agreed without more words.

Dr. Hale exhibited the house as if he owned it.

"The agent's out of town," he said, "and we don't need him anyway. He said he'd do anything you wanted, in reason."

Dr. Bellair watched with keen interest the effect of her somewhat daring description, as Miss Orella stepped from room to room examining everything with a careful eye, with an expression of growing generalship. Sue fluttered about delightedly, discovering advantages everywhere and making occasional disrespectful remarks to Vivian about Dr. Hale's clothes.

"Looks as if he never saw a clothes brush!" she said. "A finger out on his glove, a button off his coat. No need to tell us there's no woman in his house!"

"You can decide about your cook when you've tried her," he said to Miss Elder. "I engaged her for a week—on trial. She's in the kitchen now, and will have your dinner ready presently. I think you'll like her, if—"

"Good boy!" said Dr. Bellair. "Sometimes you show as much sense as a woman—almost."

"What's the 'if' " asked Miss Orella, looking worried.

"Question of character," he answered. "She's about forty-five, with a boy of sixteen or so. He's not over bright, but a willing worker. She's a good woman—from one standpoint. She won't leave that boy nor give him up to strangers; but she has a past!"

"What is her present?" Dr. Bellair asked, "that's the main thing."

Dr. Hale clapped her approvingly on the shoulder, but looked doubtingly toward Miss Orella.

"And what's her future if somebody don't help her?" Vivian urged.

"Can she cook?" asked Grandma.

"Is she a safe person to have in the house?" inquired Dr. Bellair meaningly.

"She can cook," he replied. "She's French, or of French parentage. She used to keep a little—place of entertainment. The food was excellent. She's been a patient of mine—off and on—for five years—and I should call her perfectly safe."

Miss Orella still looked worried. "I'd like to help her and the boy, but would it—look well? I don't want to be mean about it, but this is a very serious venture with us, Dr. Hale, and I have these girls with me."

"With you and Dr. Bellair and Mrs. Pettigrew the young ladies will be quite safe, Miss Elder. As to the woman's present character, she has suffered two changes of heart, she's become a religious devotee—and a man-hater! And from a business point of view, I assure you that if Jeanne Jeaune is in your kitchen you'll never have a room empty."

"Johnny Jones! queer name for a woman!" said Grandma. They repeated it to her carefully, but she only changed to "Jennie June," and adhered to one or the other, thereafter. "What's the boy's name?" she asked further.

"Theophile," Dr. Hale replied.

"Huh!" said she.

"Why don't she keep an eating-house still?" asked Dr. Bellair rather suspiciously.

"That's what I like best about her," he answered. "She is trying to break altogether with her past. She wants to give up 'public life'—and private life won't have her."

They decided to try the experiment, and found it worked well.

There were two bedrooms over the kitchen where "Mrs. Jones" as Grandma generally called her, and her boy, could be quite comfortable and by themselves; and although of a somewhat sour and unsociable aspect, and fiercely watchful lest anyone offend her son, this questionable character proved an unquestionable advantage. With the boy's help, she cooked for the houseful, which grew to be a family of twenty-five. He also wiped dishes, helped in the laundry work, cleaned and scrubbed and carried coal; and Miss Elder, seeing his steady usefulness, insisted on paying wages for him too. This unlooked for praise and gain won the mother's heart, and as she grew more at home with them, and he less timid, she encouraged him to do the heavier cleaning in the rest of the house.

"Huh!" said Grandma. "I wish more sane and moral persons would work like that!"

Vivian watched with amazement the swift filling of the house.

There was no trouble at all about boarders, except in discriminating among them. "Make them pay in advance, Rella," Dr. Bellair advised, "it doesn't cost them any more, and it is a great convenience. 'References exchanged,' of course. There are a good many here that I know—you can always count on Mr. Dykeman and Fordham Grier, and John Unwin."

Before a month was over the place was full to its limits with what Sue called "assorted boarders," the work ran smoothly and the business end of Miss Elder's venture seemed quite safe. They had the twenty Dr. Bellair prophesied, and except for her, Mrs. Pettigrew, Miss Peeder, a teacher of dancing and music, Mrs. Jocelyn, who was interested in mining, and Sarah Hart, who described herself as a "journalist," all were men.

Fifteen men to eight women. Miss Elder sat at the head of her table, looked down it and across the other one, and marvelled continuously. Never in her New England life had she been with so many men—except in church—and they were more scattered. This houseful of heavy feet and broad shoulders, these deep voices and loud laughs, the atmosphere of interchanging jests and tobacco smoke, was new to her. She hated the tobacco smoke, but that could not be helped. They did not smoke in her parlor, but the house was full of it none the less, in which constant presence she began to reverse the Irishman's well known judgment of whiskey, allowing that while all tobacco was bad, some tobacco was much worse than others.

5

CONTRASTS

Old England thinks our country
  Is a wilderness at best—
And small New England thinks the same
  Of the large free-minded West.

Some people know the good old way
  Is the only way to do,
And find there must be something wrong
  In anything that's new.

To Vivian the new life offered a stimulus, a sense of stir and promise even beyond her expectations. She wrote dutiful letters to her mother, trying to describe the difference between this mountain town and Bainville, but found the New England viewpoint an insurmountable obstacle.

To Bainville "Out West" was a large blank space on the map, and the blank space in the mind which matched it was but sparsely dotted with a few disconnected ideas such as "cowboy," "blizzard," "prairie fire," "tornado," "border ruffian," and the like.

The girl's painstaking description of the spreading, vigorous young town, with its fine, modern buildings, its banks and stores and theatres, its country club and parks, its pleasant social life, made small impression on the Bainville mind. But the fact that Miss Elder's venture was successful from the first did impress old acquaintances, and Mrs. Lane read aloud to selected visitors her daughter's accounts of their new and agreeable friends. Nothing was said of "chaps," "sombreros," or "shooting up the town," however, and therein a distinct sense of loss was felt.

Much of what was passing in Vivian's mind she could not make clear to her mother had she wished to. The daily presence and very friendly advances of so many men, mostly young and all polite (with the exception of Dr. Hale, whose indifference was almost rude by contrast), gave a new life and color to the days.

She could not help giving some thought to this varied assortment, and the carefully preserved image of Morton, already nine years dim, waxed dimmer. But she had a vague consciousness of being untrue to her ideals, or to Mrs. St. Cloud's ideals, now somewhat discredited, and did not readily give herself up to the cheerful attractiveness of the position.

Susie found no such difficulty. Her ideals were simple, and while quite within the bounds of decorum, left her plenty of room for amusement. So popular did she become, so constantly in demand for rides and walks and oft-recurring dances, that Vivian felt called upon to give elder sisterly advice.

But Miss Susan scouted her admonitions.

"Why shouldn't I have a good time?" she said. "Think how we grew up! Half a dozen boys to twenty girls, and when there was anything to go to—the lordly way they'd pick and choose! And after all our efforts and machinations most of us had to dance with each other. And the quarrels we had! Here they stand around three deep asking for dances—and *they* have to dance with each other, and *they* do the quarreling. I've heard 'em." And Sue giggled delightedly.

"There's no reason we shouldn't enjoy ourselves, Susie, of course, but aren't you—rather hard on them?"

"Oh, nonsense!" Sue protested. "Dr. Bellair said I should get married out here! She says the same old thing—that it's 'a woman's duty,' and I propose to do it. That is—they'll propose, and I won't do it! Not till I make up my mind. Now see how you like this!"

She had taken a fine large block of "legal cap" and set down their fifteen men thereon, with casual comment.

1. Mr. Unwin—Too old, big, quiet.
2. Mr. Elmer Skee—Big, too old, funny.
3. Jimmy Saunders—Middle-sized, amusing, nice.
4. P. R. Gibbs—Too little, too thin, too cocky.
5. George Waterson—Middling, pretty nice.
6. J. J. Cuthbert—Big, horrid.
7. Fordham Greer—Big, pleasant.
8. W. S. Horton—Nothing much.
9. A. L. Dykeman—Interesting, too old.
10. Professor Toomey—Little, horrid.
11. Arthur Fitzwilliam—Ridiculous, too young.
12. Howard Winchester—Too nice, distrust him.
13. Lawson W. Briggs—Nothing much.
14. Edward S. Jenks—Fair to middling.
15. Mr. A. Smith—Minus.

She held it up in triumph. "I got 'em all out of the book—quite correct. Now, which'll you have."

"Susie Elder! You little goose! Do you imagine that all these fifteen men are going to propose to you?"

"I'm sure I hope so!" said the cheerful damsel. "We've only been settled a fortnight and one of 'em has already!"

Vivian was impressed at once. "Which?—You don't mean it!"

Sue pointed to the one marked "minus."

"It was only 'A. Smith.' I never should be willing to belong to 'A. Smith,' it's too indefinite—unless it was a last resort. Several more are—well, extremely friendly! Now don't look so severe. You needn't worry about me. I'm not quite so foolish as I talk, you know."

She was not. Her words were light and saucy, but she was as demure and decorous a little New Englander as need be desired; and she could not help it if the hearts of the unattached young men of whom the town was full, warmed towards her.

Dr. Bellair astonished them at lunch one day in their first week.

"Dick Hale wants us all to come over to tea this afternoon," she said, as if it was the most natural thing in the world.

"Tea? Where?" asked Mrs. Pettigrew sharply.

"At his house. He has 'a home of his own,' you know. And he

particularly wants you, Mrs. Pettigrew—and Miss Elder—the girls, of course."

"I'm sure I don't care to go," Vivian remarked with serene indifference, but Susie did.

"Oh, come on, Vivian! It'll be so funny! A man's home!—and we may never get another chance. He's such a bear!"

Dr. Hale's big house was only across the road from theirs, standing in a large lot with bushes and trees about it.

"He's been here nine years," Dr. Bellair told them. "That's an old inhabitant for us. He boarded in that house for a while; then it was for sale and he bought it. He built that little office of his at the corner—says he doesn't like to live where he works, or work where he lives. He took his meals over here for a while—and then set up for himself."

"I should think he'd be lonely," Miss Elder suggested.

"Oh, he has his boys, you know—always three or four young fellows about him. It's a mighty good thing for them, too."

Dr. Hale's home proved a genuine surprise. They had regarded it as a big, neglected-looking place, and found on entering the gate that the inside view of that rampant shrubbery was extremely pleasant. Though not close cut and swept of leaves and twigs, it still was beautiful; and the tennis court and tether-ball ring showed the ground well used.

Grandma looked about her with a keen interrogative eye, and was much impressed, as, indeed, were they all. She voiced their feelings justly when, the true inwardness of this pleasant home bursting fully upon them, she exclaimed:

"Well, of all things! A man keeping house!"

"Why not?" asked Dr. Hale with his dry smile. "Is there any deficiency, mental or physical, about a man, to prevent his attempting this abstruse art?"

She looked at him sharply. "I don't know about deficiency, but there seems to be somethin' about 'em that keeps 'em out of the business. I guess it's because women are so cheap."

"No doubt you are right, Mrs. Pettigrew. And here women are scarce and high. Hence my poor efforts."

His poor efforts had bought or built a roomy pleasant house, and furnished it with a solid comfort and calm attractiveness that was most satisfying. Two Chinamen did the work; cooking, cleaning, washing, waiting on table, with silent efficiency. "They are as steady as eight-day clocks," said Dr. Hale. "I pay them good wages and they are worth it."

"Sun here had to go home once—to be married, also, to see his honored parents, I believe, and to leave a grand-'Sun' to attend to the ancestors; but he brought in another Chink first and trained him so well that I hardly noticed the difference. Came back in a year or so, and resumed his place without a jar."

Miss Elder watched with fascinated eyes these soft-footed servants with clean, white garments and shiny coils of long, braided hair.

"I may have to come to it," she admitted, "but—dear me, it doesn't seem natural to have a man doing housework!"

Dr. Hale smiled again. "You don't want men to escape from dependence, I see. Perhaps, if more men knew how comfortably they could live without women, the world would be happier." There was a faint wire-edge to his tone, in spite of the courteous expression, but Miss Elder did not notice it and if Mrs. Pettigrew did, she made no comment.

They noted the varied excellences of his housekeeping with high approval.

"You certainly know how, Dr. Hale," said Miss Orella; "I particularly admire these beds—with the sheets buttoned down, German fashion, isn't it? What made you do that?"

"I've slept so much in hotels," he answered; "and found the sheets always inadequate to cover the blankets—and the marks of other men's whiskers! I don't like blankets in my neck. Besides it saves washing."

Mrs. Pettigrew nodded vehemently. "You have sense," she said.

The labor-saving devices were a real surprise to them. A "chute" for soiled clothing shot from the bathroom on each floor to the laundry in the basement; a dumbwaiter of construction large and strong enough to carry trunks, went from cellar to roof; the fireplaces dropped their ashes down mysterious inner holes; and for the big one in the living-room a special "lift" raised a box of wood up to the floor level, hidden by one of the "settles."

"Saves work—saves dirt—saves expense," said Dr. Hale.

Miss Orella and her niece secretly thought the rooms rather bare, but Dr. Bellair was highly in favor of that very feature.

"You see Dick don't believe in jimcracks and dirt-catchers, and he likes sunlight. Books all under glass—no curtains to wash and darn and fuss with—none of those fancy pincushions and embroidered thingummies—I quite envy him."

"Why don't you have one yourself, Johnny?" he asked her.

"Because I don't like housekeeping," she said, "and you do. Masculine instinct, I suppose!"

"Huh!" said Mrs. Pettigrew with her sudden one-syllable chuckle.

The girls followed from room to room, scarce noticing these comments, or the eager politeness of the four pleasant-faced young fellows who formed the doctor's present family. She could not but note the intelligent efficiency of the place, but felt more deeply the underlying spirit, the big-brotherly kindness which prompted his hospitable care of these nice boys. It was delightful to hear them praise him.

"O, he's simply great," whispered Archie Burns, a ruddy-cheeked young Scotchman. "He pretends there's nothing to it—that he wants company—that we pay for all we get—and that sort of thing, you know; but this is no boarding house, I can tell you!" And then he flushed till his very hair grew redder—remembering that the guests came from one.

"Of course not!" Vivian cordially agreed with him. "You must have lovely times here. I don't wonder you appreciate it!" and she smiled so sweetly that he felt at ease again.

Beneath all this cheery good will and the gay chatter of the group her quick sense caught an impression of something hidden and repressed. She felt the large and quiet beauty of the rooms; the smooth comfort, the rational, pleasant life; but still more she felt a deep keynote of loneliness.

The pictures told her most. She noted one after another with inward comment.

"There's 'Persepolis,' " she said to herself—"loneliness incarnate; and that other lion-and-ruin thing,—loneliness and decay. Gerome's 'Lion in the Desert,' too, the same thing. Then Daniel—more lions, more loneliness, but power. 'Circe and the Companions of Ulysses'—cruel, but loneliness and power again—of a sort. There's that 'Island of Death' too—a beautiful thing—but O dear!—And young Burne-Jones' 'Vampire' was in one of the bedrooms—that one he shut the door of!"

While they ate and drank in the long, low-ceiled wide-windowed room below, she sought the bookcases and looked them over curiously. Yes—there was Marcus Aurelius, Epictetus, Plato, Emerson and Carlisle—the great German philosophers, the French, the English—all showing signs of use.

Dr. Hale observed her inspection. It seemed to vaguely annoy him, as if someone were asking too presuming questions.

"Interested in philosophy, Miss Lane?" he asked, drily, coming toward her.

"Yes—so far as I understand it," she answered.

"And how far does that go?"

She felt the inference, and raised her soft eyes to his rather reproachfully.

"Not far, I am afraid. But I do know that these books teach one how to bear trouble."

He met her gaze steadily, but something seemed to shut, deep in his eyes. They looked as unassailable as a steel safe. He straightened his big shoulders with a defiant shrug, and returned to sit by Mrs. Pettigrew, to whom he made himself most agreeable.

The four young men did the honors of the tea table, with devotion to all; and some especially intended for the younger ladies. Miss Elder cried out in delight at the tea.

"Where did you get it, Dr. Hale? Can it be had here?"

"I'm afraid not. That is a particular brand. Sun brought me a chest of it when he came from his visit."

When they went home each lady was given a present, Chinese fashion—lychee nuts for Sue, lily-bulbs for Vivian, a large fan for Mrs. Pettigrew, and a package of the wonderful tea for Miss Orella.

"That's a splendid thing for him to do," she said, as they walked back. "Such a safe place for those boys!"

"It's lovely of him," Sue agreed. "I don't care if he is a woman-hater."

Vivian said nothing, but admitted, on being questioned, that "he was very interesting."

Mrs. Pettigrew was delighted with their visit. "I like this country," she declared. "Things are different. A man couldn't do that in Bainville—he'd be talked out of town."

That night she sought Dr. Bellair and questioned her.

"Tell me about that man," she demanded. "How old is he?"

"Not as old as he looks by ten years," said the doctor. "No, I can't tell you why his hair's gray."

"What woman upset him?" asked the old lady.

Dr. Bellair regarded her thoughtfully. "He has made me no confidences, Mrs. Pettigrew, but I think you are right. It must have been a severe shock—for he is very bitter against women. It is a shame, too, for he is one of the best of men. He prefers men patients—and gets them. The women he will treat if he must, but he is kindest to the 'fallen' ones, and inclined to sneer at the rest. And yet he's the straightest man I ever knew. I'm thankful to have him come here so much. He needs it."

Mrs. Pettigrew marched off, nodding sagely. She felt a large and growing interest in her new surroundings, more especially in the numerous boys, but was somewhat amazed at her popularity among them. These young men were mainly exiles from home; the older ones, though more settled perhaps, had been even longer away from their early surroundings; and a real live Grandma, as Jimmy Saunders said, was an "attraction."

"If you were mine," he told her laughingly, "I'd get a pianist and some sort of little side show, and exhibit you all up and down the mountains!—for good money. Why some of the boys never had a Grandma, and those that did haven't seen one since they were kids!"

"Very complimentary, I'm sure—but impracticable," said the old lady.

The young men came to her with confidences, they asked her advice, they kept her amused with tales of their adventures; some true, some greatly diversified; and she listened with a shrewd little smile and a wag of the head—so they never were quite sure whether they were "fooling" Grandma or not.

To her, as a general confidant, came Miss Peeder with a tale of woe. The little hall that she rented for her dancing classes had burned down on a windy Sunday, and there was no other suitable and within her means.

"There's Sloan's; but it's over a barroom—it's really not possible.

And Baker's is too expensive. The church rooms they won't let for dancing—I don't know what I *am* to do, Mrs. Pettigrew!"

"Why don't you ask Orella Elder to rent you her dining-room—it's big enough. They could move the tables—"

Miss Peeder's eyes opened in hopeful surprise. "Oh, if she *would! Do you* think she would? It would be ideal."

Miss Elder being called upon, was quite fluttered by the proposition, and consulted Dr. Bellair.

"Why not?" said that lady. "Dancing is first rate exercise—good for us all. Might as well have the girls dance here under your eye as going out all the time—and it's some addition to the income. They'll pay extra for refreshments, too. I'd do it."

With considerable trepidation Miss Orella consented, and their first "class night" was awaited by her in a state of suppressed excitement.

To have music and dancing—"with refreshments"—twice a week—in her own house—this seemed to her like a career of furious dissipation.

Vivian, though with a subtle sense of withdrawal from a too general intimacy, was inwardly rather pleased; and Susie bubbled over with delight.

"Oh what fun!" she cried. "I never had enough dancing! I don't believe anybody has!"

"We don't belong to the Class, you know," Vivian reminded her.

"Oh yes! Miss Peeder says we must *all* come—that she would feel *very* badly if we didn't; and the boarders have all joined—to a man!"

Everyone seemed pleased except Mrs. Jeaune. Dancing she considered immoral; music, almost as much so—and Miss Elder trembled lest she lose her. But the offer of extra payments for herself and son on these two nights each week proved sufficient to quell her scruples.

Theophile doubled up the tables, set chairs around the walls, waxed the floor, and was then sent to bed and locked in by his anxious mother.

She labored, during the earlier hours of the evening, in the preparation of sandwiches and coffee, cake and lemonade—which viands were later shoved through the slide by the austere cook, and distributed as from a counter by Miss Peeder's assistant. Mrs. Jeaune would come no nearer, but peered darkly upon them through the peephole in the swinging door.

It was a very large room, due to the time when many "mealers" had been accommodated. There were windows on each side, windows possessing the unusual merit of opening from the top; wide double doors made the big front hall a sort of anteroom, and the stairs and piazza furnished opportunities for occasional couples who felt the wish for retirement. In the right-angled passages, long hatracks on either side were hung with "Derbies," "Kossuths" and "Stetsons," and the ladies took off their wraps, and added finishing touches to their toilettes in Miss Elder's room.

The house was full of stir and bustle, of pretty dresses, of giggles and whispers, and the subdued exchange of comments among the gentlemen. The men predominated, so that there was no lack of partners for any of the ladies.

Miss Orella accepted her new position with a half-terrified enjoyment. Not in many years had she found herself so in demand. Her always neat and appropriate costume had blossomed suddenly for the occasion; her hair, arranged by the affectionate and admiring Susie, seemed softer and more voluminous. Her eyes grew brilliant, and the delicate color in her face warmed and deepened.

Miss Peeder had installed a pianola to cover emergencies, but on this opening evening she had both piano and violin—good, lively, sole-stirring music. Everyone was on the floor, save a few gentlemen who evidently wished they were.

Sue danced with the gaiety and lightness of a kitten among windblown leaves, Vivian with gliding grace, smooth and harmonious, Miss Orella with skill and evident enjoyment, though still conscientious in every accurate step.

Presently Mrs. Pettigrew appeared, sedately glorious in black silk, jet-beaded, and with much fine old lace. She bore in front of her a small wicker rocking chair, and headed for a corner near the door. Her burden was promptly taken from her by one of the latest comers, a tall person with a most devoted manner.

"Allow *me,* ma'am," he said, and placed the little chair at the point she indicated. "No lady ought to rustle for rockin' chairs with so many gentlemen present."

He was a man of somewhat advanced age, but his hair was still more black than white and had a curly, wiggish effect save as its indigenous character was proven by three small bare patches of a conspicuous nature.

He bowed so low before her that she could not help observing these distinctions, and then answered her startled look before she had time to question him.

"Yes'm," he explained, passing his hand over head; "scalped three several times and left for dead. But I'm here yet. Mr. Elmer Skee, at your service."

"I thought when an Indian scalped you there wasn't enough hair left to make Greeley whiskers," said Grandma, rising to the occasion.

"Oh, no, ma'am, they ain't so efficacious as all that—not in these parts. I don't know what the ancient Mohawks may have done, but the Apaches only want a patch—smaller to carry and just as good to show off. They're collectors, you know—like a phil-e-a-to-lol-o-gist!"

"Skee, did you say?" pursued the old lady, regarding him with interest and convinced that there was something wrong with the name of that species of collector.

"Yes'm. Skee—Elmer Skee. No'm, *not* pronounced 'she.' Do I look like it?"

Mr. Skee was an interesting relic of that stormy past of the once Wild West which has left so few surviving. He had crossed the plains as a child, he told her, in the days of the prairie schooner, had then and there lost his parents and his first bit of scalp, was picked up alive by a party of "movers," and had grown up in a playground of sixteen states and territories.

Grandma gazed upon him fascinated. "I judge you might be interesting to talk with," she said, after he had given her this brief sketch of his youth.

"Thank you, ma'am," said Mr. Skee. "May I have the pleasure of this dance?"

"I haven't danced in thirty years," said she, dubitating.

"The more reason for doing it now," he calmly insisted.

"Why not?" said Mrs. Pettigrew, and they forthwith executed a species of march, the gentleman pacing with the elaborate grace of a circus horse, and Grandma stepping at his side with great decorum.

Later on, warming to the occasion, Mr. Skee frisked and high-stepped with the youngest and gayest, and found the supper so wholly to his liking that he promptly applied for a room, and as soon as one was vacant it was given to him.

Vivian danced to her heart's content and enjoyed the friendly merriment about her; but when Fordham Greer took her out on the long piazza to rest and breathe a little, she saw the dark bulk of the house across the street and the office with its half-lit window, and could not avoid thinking of the lonely man there.

He had not come to the dance, no one expected that, of course; but all his boys had come and were having the best of times.

"It's his own fault, of course; but it's a shame," she thought.

The music sounded gaily from within, and young Greer urged for another dance.

She stood there for a moment, hesitating, her hand on his arm, when a tall figure came briskly up the street from the station, turned in at their gate, came up the steps—

The girl gave a little cry, and shrank back for an instant, then eagerly came forward and gave her hand to him.

It was Morton.

6

NEW FRIENDS AND OLD

'Twould be too bad to be true, my dear,
    And wonders never cease;
'Twould be too bad to be true, my dear,
    If all one's swans were geese!

Vivian's startled cry of welcome was heard by Susie, perched on the stairs with several eager youths gathered as close as might be about her, and several pairs of hands helped her swift descent to greet her brother.

Miss Orella, dropping Mr. Dykeman's arm, came flying from the ball-room.

"Oh, Morton! Morton! When did you come? Why didn't you let us know? Oh, my *dear* boy!"

She haled him into their special parlor, took his hat away from him, pulled out the most comfortable chair.

"Have you had supper? And to think that we haven't a room for you! But there's to be one vacant—next week. I'll see that there is. You shall have my room, dear boy. Oh, I am so glad to see you!"

Susie gave him a sisterly hug, while he kissed her, somewhat gingerly, on the cheek, and then she perched herself on the arm of a chair and gazed upon him with affectionate interest. Vivian gazed also, busily engaged in fitting present facts to past memories.

Surely he had not looked just like that! The Morton of her girlhood's dream had a clear complexion, a bright eye, a brave and gallant look—the voice only had not changed.

But here was Morton in present fact, something taller, it seemed, and a good deal heavier, well dressed in a rather vivid way, and making merry over his aunt's devotion.

"Well, if it doesn't seem like old times to have Aunt 'Rella running 'round like a hen with her head cut off, to wait on me." The simile was not unjust, though certainly ungracious, but his aunt was far too happy to resent it.

"You sit right still!" she said. "I'll go and bring you some supper. You must be hungry."

"Now do sit down and hear to reason, Auntie!" he said, reaching out a detaining hand and pulling her into a seat beside him. "I'm not hungry a little bit; had a good feed on the diner. Never mind about the room—I don't know how long I can stay—and I left my grip at the Allen House anyway. How well you're looking, Auntie! I declare I'd hardly have known you! And here's little Susie—a regular belle! And Vivian—don't suppose I dare call you Vivian now, Miss Lane?"

Vivian gave a little embarrassed laugh. If he had used her first name she would never have noticed it. Now that he asked her, she hardly knew what answer to make, but presently said:

"Why, of course, I always call you Morton."

"Well, I'll come when you call me," he cheerfully replied, leaning forward, elbows on knees, and looking around the pretty room.

"How well you're fixed here. Guess it was a wise move, Aunt 'Rella. But I'd never have dreamed you'd do it. Your Dr. Bellair must have been a powerful promoter to get you all out here. I wouldn't have thought anybody in Bainville could move—but me. Why, there's Grandma, as I live!" and he made a low bow.

Mrs. Pettigrew, hearing of his arrival from the various would-be partners of the two girls, had come to the door and stood there regarding him with a non-committal expression. At this address she frowned perceptibly.

"My name is Mrs. Pettigrew, young man. I've known you since you were a scallawag in short pants, but I'm no Grandma of yours."

"A thousand pardons! Please excuse me, Mrs. Pettigrew," he said with exaggerated politeness. "Won't you be seated?" And he set a chair for her with a flourish.

"Thanks, no," she said. "I'll go back," and went back forthwith, attended by Mr. Skee.

"One of these happy family reunions, ma'am?" he asked with approving interest. "If there's one thing I do admire, it's a happy surprise."

" 'Tis some of a surprise," Mrs. Pettigrew admitted, and became rather glum, in spite of Mr. Skee's undeniably entertaining conversation.

"Some sort of a fandango going on?" Morton asked after a few rather stiff moments. "Don't let me interrupt! On with the dance! Let joy be unconfined! And if she must"—he looked at Vivian, and went on somewhat lamely—"dance, why not dance with me? May I have the pleasure, Miss Lane?"

"Oh, no," cried Miss Orella, "we'd much rather be with you!"

"But I'd rather dance than talk, any time," said he, and crooked his elbow to Vivian with an impressive bow.

Somewhat uncertain in her own mind, and unwilling to again disappoint Fordham Greer, who had already lost one dance and was visibly waiting for her in the hall, the girl hesitated; but Susie said, "Go on, give him part of one. I'll tell Mr. Greer." So Vivian took Morton's proffered arm and returned to the floor.

She had never danced with him in the old days; no special memory was here to contrast with the present; yet something seemed vaguely wrong. He danced well, but more actively than she admired, and during the rest of the evening devoted himself to the various ladies with an air of long usage.

She was glad when the dancing was over and he had finally departed for his hotel, glad when Susie had at last ceased chattering and dropped reluctantly to sleep.

For a long time she lay awake trying to straighten out things in her mind and account to herself for the sense of vague confusion which oppressed her.

Morton had come back! That was the prominent thing, of which she repeatedly assured herself. How often she had looked forward to that moment, and felt in anticipation a vivid joy. She had thought of it in a hundred ways, always with pleasure, but never in this particular way—among so many strangers.

It must be that which confused her, she thought, for she was extremely sensitive to the attitude of those about her. She felt an unspoken criticism of Morton on the part of her new friends in the house, and resented it; yet in her own mind a faint comparison would obtrude itself between his manners and those of Jimmie Saunders or Mr. Greer, for instance. The young Scotchman she had seen regarding Morton with an undisguised dislike, and this she inwardly resented, even while herself disliking his bearing to his aunt—and to her grandmother.

It was all contradictory and unsatisfying, and she fell asleep saying over to herself, "He has come back! He has come back!" and trying to feel happy.

Aunt Orella was happy at any rate. She would not rest until her beloved nephew was installed in the house, practically turning out Mr. Gibbs in order to accommodate him. Morton protested, talked of business and of having to go away at any time; and Mr. Gibbs, who still "mealed" with them, secretly wished he would.

But Morton did not go away. It was a long time since he had been petted and waited on, and he enjoyed it hugely, treating his aunt with a serio-comic affection that was sometimes funny, sometimes disagreeable.

At least Susie found it so. Her first surprise over, she fell back on a fund of sound common sense, strengthened by present experience, and found a good deal to criticise in her returned brother. She was so young when he left, and he had teased her so unmercifully in those days, that her early memories of him were rather mixed in sentiment, and now he appeared, not as the unquestioned idol of a manless family in a well-nigh manless town, but as one among many; and of those many several were easily his superiors.

He was her brother, and she loved him, of course; but there were so many wanting to be "brothers" if not more, and they were so much more polite! Morton petted, patronized and teased her, and she took it all in good part, as after the manner of brothers, but his demeanor with other people was not to her mind.

His adoring aunt, finding no fault whatever with this well-loved nephew, lavished upon him the affection of her unused motherhood, and he seemed to find it a patent joke, open to everyone, that she should be so fond.

To this and, indeed, to his general walk and conversation, Mrs. Pettigrew took great exception.

"Fine boy—Rella's nephew!" she said to Dr. Bellair late one night when, seeing a light over her neighbor's transom, she dropped in for a little chat. Conversation seemed easier for her here than in the atmosphere of Bainville.

"Fine boy—eh? Nice complexion!"

Dr. Bellair was reading a heavy-weight book by a heavier-weight specialist. She laid it down, took off her eyeglasses, and rubbed them.

"Better not kiss him," she said.

"I though as much!" said Grandma. "I *thought* as much! Huh!"

"Nice world, isn't it?" the doctor suggested genially.

"Nothing the matter with the world, that I know of," her visitor answered.

"Nice people, then—how's that?"

"Nothing the matter with the people but foolishness—plain foolishness. Good land! Shall we *never* learn anything!"

"Not till it's too late apparently," the doctor gloomily agreed, turning slowly in her swivel chair. "That boy never was taught anything to protect him. What did Rella know? Or for that matter, what do any boys' fathers and mothers know? Nothing, you'd think. If they do, they won't teach it to their children."

"Time they did!" said the old lady decidedly. "High time they did! It's never too late to learn. I've learned a lot out of you and your books, Jane Bellair. Interesting reading! I don't suppose you could give an absolute opinion now, could you?"

"No," said Dr. Bellair gravely, "no, I couldn't; not yet, anyway."

"Well, we've got to keep our eyes open," Mrs. Pettigrew concluded. "When I think of that girl of mine—"

"Yes—or any girl," the doctor added.

"You look out for any girl—that's your business; I'll look out for mine—if I can."

Mrs. Pettigrew's were not the only eyes to scrutinize Morton Elder. Through the peep-hole in the swing door to the kitchen, Jeanne Jeaune watched him darkly with one hand on her lean chest.

She kept her watch on whatever went on in that dining-room, and on the two elderly waitresses whom she had helped Miss Elder to secure when the house filled up. They were rather painfully unattractive, but seemed likely to stay where no young and pretty damsel could be counted on for a year. Morton joked with perseverance about their looks, and those who were most devoted to Susie seemed to admire his wit, while Vivian's special admirers found it pointless in the extreme.

"Your waitresses are the limit, Auntie," he said, "but the cook is all to the good. Is she a plain cook or a handsome one?"

"Handsome is as handsome does, young man," Mrs. Pettigrew pointedly replied. "Mrs. Jones is a first-class cook and her looks are neither here nor there."

"You fill me with curiosity," he replied. "I must go out and make her acquaintance. I always get solid with the cook; it's worth while."

The face at the peep-hole darkened and turned away with a bitter and determined look, and Master Theophile was hastened at his work till his dim intelligence wondered, and then blessed with an unexpected cookie.

Vivian, Morton watched and followed assiduously. She was much changed from what he remembered—the young, frightened, slender girl he had kissed under the lilac bushes, a kiss long since forgotten among many.

Perhaps the very number of his subsequent acquaintances during a varied and not markedly successful career in the newer states made this type of New England womanhood more marked. Girls he had known of various sorts, women old and young had been kind to him, for Morton had the rough good looks and fluent manner which easily find their way to the good will of many female hearts; but this gentle refinement of manner and delicate beauty had a novel charm for him.

Sitting by his aunt at meals he studied Vivian opposite, he watched her in their few quiet evenings together, under the soft lamplight on Miss Elder's beloved "center table;" and studied her continually in the stimulating presence of many equally devoted men.

All that was best in him was stirred by her quiet grace, her reserved friendliness; and the spur of rivalry was by no means wanting. Both the girls had their full share of masculine attention in that busy houseful, each having her own particular devotees, and the position of comforter to the others.

Morton became openly devoted to Vivian, and followed her about, seeking every occasion to be alone with her, a thing difficult to accomplish.

"I don't ever get a chance to see anything of you," he said. "Come on, take a walk with me—won't you?"

"You can see me all day, practically," she answered. "It seems to me that I never saw a man with so little to do."

"Now that's too bad, Vivian! Just because a fellow's out of a job for a while! It isn't the first time, either; in my business you work like—like anything, part of the time, and then get laid off. I work hard enough when I'm at it."

"Do you like it—that kind of work?" the girl asked.

They were sitting in the family parlor, but the big hall was as usual well occupied, and some one or more of the boarders always eager to come in. Miss Elder at this moment had departed for special conference with her cook, and Susie was at the theatre with Jimmie Saunders. Fordham Greer had asked Vivian, as had Morton also, but she declined both on the ground that she didn't like that kind of play. Mrs. Pettigrew, being joked too persistently about her fondness for "long whist," had retired to her room—but then, her room was divided from the parlor only by a thin partition and a door with a most inefficacious latch.

"Come over here by the fire," said Morton, "and I'll tell you all about it."

He seated himself on a sofa, comfortably adjacent to the fireplace, but Vivian preferred a low rocker.

"I suppose you mean travelling—and selling goods?" he pursued. "Yes, I like it. There's lots of change—and you meet people. I'd hate to be shut up in an office."

"But do you—get anywhere with it? Is there any outlook for you? Anything worth doing?"

"There's a good bit of money to be made, if you mean that; that is, if a fellow's a good salesman. I'm no slouch myself, when I feel in the mood. But it's easy come, easy go, you see. And it's uncertain. There are times like this, with nothing doing."

"I didn't mean money, altogether," said the girl meditatively, "but the work itself; I don't see any future for you."

Morton was pleased with her interest. Reaching between his knees he seized the edge of the small sofa and dragged it a little nearer, quite unconscious that the act was distasteful to her.

Though twenty-five years old, Vivian was extremely young in many ways, and her introspection had spent itself in tending the inner shrine of his early image. That ikon was now jarringly displaced by this insistent presence, and she could not satisfy herself yet as to whether the change pleased or displeased her. Again and again his manner antagonized her, but his visible devotion carried an undeniable appeal, and his voice stirred the deep well of emotion in her heart.

"Look here, Vivian," he said, "you've no idea how it goes through me to have you speak like that! You see I've been knocking around here for all this time, and I haven't had a soul to take an interest. A fellow needs the society of good women—like you."

It is an old appeal, and always reaches the mark. To any woman it is a compliment, and to a young girl, doubly alluring. As she looked at him, the very things she most disliked, his too free manner, his coarsened complexion, a certain look about the eyes, suddenly assumed a new interest as proofs of his loneliness and lack of right companionship. What Mrs. St. Cloud had told her of the ennobling influence of a true woman, flashed upon her mind.

"You see, I had no mother," he said simply—"and Aunt Rella spoiled me—." He looked now like the boy she used to know.

"Of course I ought to have behaved better," he admitted. "I was ungrateful—I can see it now. But it did seem to me I couldn't stand that town a day longer!"

She could sympathize with this feeling and showed it.

"Then when a fellow knocks around as I have so long, he gets to where he doesn't care a hang for anything. Seeing you again makes a lot of difference, Vivian. I think, perhaps—I could take a new start."

"Oh do! Do!" she said eagerly. "You're young enough, Morton. You can do anything if you'll make up your mind to it."

"And you'll help me?"

"Of course I'll help you—if I can," said she.

A feeling of sincere remorse for wasted opportunities rose in the young man's mind; also, in the presence of this pure-eyed girl, a sense of shame for his previous habits. He walked to the window, his hands in his pockets, and looked out blankly for a moment.

"A fellow does a lot of things he shouldn't," he began, clearing his throat; she met him more than half way with the overflowing generosity of youth and ignorance:

"Never mind what you've done, Morton—you're going to do differently now! Susie'll be so proud of you—and Aunt Orella!"

"And you?" He turned upon her suddenly.

"Oh—I? Of course! I shall be very proud of my old friend."

She met his eyes bravely, with a lovely look of hope and courage, and again his heart smote him.

"I hope you will," he said and straightened his broad shoulders manfully.

"Morton Elder!" cried his aunt, bustling in with deep concern in her voice, "What's this I hear about you're having a sore throat?"

"Nothing, I hope," said he cheerfully.

"Now, Morton"—Vivian showed new solicitude—"you know you have got a sore throat; Susie told me."

"Well, I wish she'd hold her tongue," he protested. "It's nothing at all—be all right in a jiffy. No, I won't take any of your fixings, Auntie."

"I want Dr. Bellair to look at it anyhow," said his aunt, anxiously. "She'll know if it's diphtheritic or anything. She's coming in."

"She can just go out again," he said with real annoyance. "If there's anything I've no use for it's a woman doctor!"

"Oh hush, hush!" cried Vivian, too late.

"Don't apologize," said Dr. Bellair from her doorway. "I'm not in the least offended. Indeed, I had rather surmised that that was your attitude; I didn't come in to prescribe, but to find Mrs. Pettigrew."

"Want me?" inquired the old lady from her doorway. "Who's got a sore throat?"

"Morton has," Vivian explained, "and he won't let Aunt Rella—why where is she?"

Miss Elder had gone out as suddenly as she had entered.

"Camphor's good for sore throat," Mrs. Pettigrew volunteered. "Three or four drops on a piece of sugar. Is it the swelled kind, or the kind that smarts?"

"Oh—Halifax!" exclaimed Morton, disgustedly. "It isn't *any* kind. I haven't a sore throat."

"Camphor's good for cold sores; you have one of them anyhow," the old lady persisted, producing a little bottle and urging it upon Morton. "Just keep it wet with camphor as often as you think of it, and it'll go away."

Vivian looked on, interested and sympathetic, but Morton put his hand to his lip and backed away.

"If you ladies don't stop trying to doctor me, I'll clear out to-morrow, so there!"

This appalling threat was fortunately unheard by his aunt, who popped in again at this moment, dragging Dr. Hale with her. Dr. Bellair smiled quietly to herself.

"I wouldn't tell him what I wanted him for, or he wouldn't have come, I'm sure—doctors are so funny," said Miss Elder, breathlessly, "but here he is. Now, Dr. Hale, here's a foolish boy who won't listen to reason, and I'm real worried about him. I want you to look at his throat."

Dr. Hale glanced briefly at Morton's angry face.

"The patient seems to be of age, Miss Elder; and, if you'll excuse me, does not seem to have authorized this call."

"My affectionate family are bound to have me an invalid," Morton explained. "I'm in imminent danger of hot baths, cold presses, mustard plasters, aconite, belladonna and quinine—and if I can once reach my hat—"

He sidled to the door and fled in mock terror.

"Thank you for your good intentions, Miss Elder," Dr. Hale remarked drily. "You can bring water to the horse, but you can't make him drink it, you see."

"Now that that young man has gone we might have a game of whist," Mrs. Pettigrew suggested, looking not ill-pleased.

"For which you do not need me in the least," and Dr. Hale was about to leave, but Dr. Bellair stopped him.

"Don't be an everlasting Winter woodchuck, Dick! Sit down and play; do be good. I've got to see old Mrs. Graham yet; she refuses to go to sleep without it—knowing I'm so near. By by."

Mrs. Pettigrew insisted on playing with Miss Elder, so Vivian had the questionable pleasure of Dr. Hale as a partner. He was an expert, used to frequent and scientific play, and by no means patient with the girl's mistakes.

He made no protest at a lost trick, but explained briefly between hands what she should have remembered and how the cards lay, till she grew quite discouraged.

Her game was but mediocre, played only to oblige; and she never could see why people cared so much about a mere pastime. Pride came to her rescue at last; the more he criticised, the more determined she grew to profit by all this advice; but her mind would wander now and then to Morton, to his young life so largely wasted, it appeared, and to what hope might lie before him. Could she be the help and stimulus he seemed to think? How much did he mean by asking her to help him?

"Why waste a thirteenth trump on your partner's thirteenth card?" Dr. Hale was asking.

She flushed a deep rose color and lifted appealing eyes to him.

"Do forgive me; my mind was elsewhere."

"Will you not invite it to return?" he suggested drily.

He excused himself after a few games, and the girl at last was glad to have him go. She wanted to be alone with her thoughts.

Mrs. Pettigrew, sitting unaccountably late at her front window, watched the light burn steadily in the small office at the opposite corner. Presently she saw a familiar figure slip in there, and, after a considerable stay, come out quietly, cross the street, and let himself in at their door.

"Huh!" said Mrs. Pettigrew.

7

SIDE LIGHTS

High shines the golden shield in front,
  To those who are not blind;
    And clear and bright
    In all men's sight,
  The silver shield behind.

In breadth and sheen each face is seen;
  How tall it is, how wide;
    But its thinness shows
    To only those
  Who stand on either side.

Theophile wept aloud in the dining-room, nursing one hand in the other, like a hurt monkey.

Most of the diners had departed, but Professor Toomey and Mr. Cuthbert still lingered about Miss Susie's corner, to the evident displeasure of Mr. Saunders, who lingered also.

Miss Susie smiled upon them all; and Mr. Saunders speculated endlessly as to whether this was due to her general friendliness of disposition, to an interest in pleasing her aunt's boarders, to personal preference, or, as he sometimes imagined, to a desire to tease him.

Morton was talking earnestly with Vivian at the other end of the table, from which the two angular waitresses had some time since removed the last plate. One of them opened the swing door a crack and thrust her head in.

"He's burnt his hand," she said, "and his Ma's out. We don't dare go near him." Both of these damsels professed great terror of the poor boy, though he was invariably good natured, and as timid as a rabbit.

"Do get the doctor!" cried Susie, nervously; she never felt at ease with Theophile.

"Dr. Bellair, I fear, is not in her office," Professor Toomey announced. "We might summon Dr. Hale."

"Nonsense!" said Mr. Cuthbert, rising heavily. "He's a great baby, that's all. Here! Quit that howling and show me your hand!"

He advanced upon Theophile, who fled toward Vivian. Morton rose in her defence. "Get out!" he said, "Go back to the kitchen. There's nothing the matter with you."

"Wait till you get burned, and see if you think it's nothing," Jimmy Saunders remarked with some acidity. He did not like Mr. Elder. "Come here youngster, let me see it."

But the boy was afraid of all of them, and cowered in a corner, still bawling. "Stop your noise," Mr. Cuthbert shouted, "Get out of this, or I'll put you out."

Vivian rose to her feet. "You will do nothing of the kind. If you, all of you, will go away, I can quiet Theophile, myself."

Susie went promptly. She had every confidence in her friend's management. Mr. Cuthbert was sulky, but followed Susie; and Mr. Saunders, after some hesitation, followed Susie, too.

Morton lingered, distrustful.

"Please go, Morton. I know how to manage him. Just leave us alone," Vivian urged.

"You'd better let me put him out, and keep him out, till the old woman comes back," Morton insisted.

"You mean kindly, I don't doubt, but you're making me very angry," said the girl, flushing; and he reluctantly left the room. Professor Toomey had departed long since, to fulfill his suggestion of calling Dr. Hale, but when that gentleman appeared, he found that Vivian had quieted the boy, stayed him with flagons and comforted him with apples, as it were, and bound up his hand in wet cooking soda.

"It's not a very bad burn," she told the doctor, "but it hurt, and he was frightened. He is afraid of everybody but his mother, and the men were cross to him."

"I see," said Dr. Hale, watching Theophile as he munched his apple, keeping carefully behind Vivian and very near her. "He does not seem much afraid of you, I notice, and he's used to me. The soda is all right. Where did you learn first aid to the injured, and how to handle—persons of limited understanding?"

"The former I studied. The latter comes by nature, I think," replied the girl, annoyed.

He laughed, rather suddenly. "It's a good quality, often needed in this world."

"What's all this rumpus?" demanded Grandma, appearing at the door. "Waking me up out of my nap!" Grandma's smooth, fine, still dark hair, which she wore in "water waves," was somewhat disarranged, and she held a little shawl about her.

"Only the household baby, playing with fire," Dr. Hale answered. "Miss Lane resolved herself into a Red Cross society, and attended to the wounded. However I think I'll have a look at it now I'm here."

Then was Vivian surprised, and compelled to admiration, to see with what wise gentleness the big man won the confidence of the frightened boy, examined the hurt hand, and bound it up again.

"You'll do, all right, won't you Theophile," he said, and offered him a shining nickel and a lozenge, "Which will you have, old man?"

After some cautious hesitation the boy chose the lozenge, and hastily applied it where it would do the most good.

"Where's Mrs. Jones all this time?" suddenly demanded Grandma, who had gone back to her room and fetched forth three fat, pink gumdrops for the further consolation of the afflicted.

"She had to go out to buy clothes for him, she hardly ever leaves him you know," Vivian explained. "And the girls out there are so afraid that they won't take any care of him."

This was true enough, but Vivian did not know that "Mrs. Jones" had returned and, peering through her favorite peephole, had seen her send out the others, and attend to the boy's burn with her own hand. Jeanne Jeaune was not a sentimental person, and judged from her son's easy consolation that he was little hurt, but she watched the girl's prompt tenderness with tears in her eyes.

"She regards him as any other boy;" thought the mother. "His infirmity, she does not recall it." Dr. Hale had long since won her approval, and when Theophile at last ran out, eager to share his gumdrops, he found her busy as usual in the kitchen.

She was a silent woman, professionally civil to the waitresses, but never cordial. The place pleased her, she was saving money, and she knew that there must be *some* waitresses—these were probably no worse than others. For her unfortunate son she expected little, and strove to keep him near her so far as possible; but Vivian's real kindness touched her deeply.

She kept a sharp eye on whatever went on in the dining-room, and what with the frequent dances and the little groups which used to hang about the table after meals, or fill a corner of the big room for quiet chats, she had good opportunities.

Morton's visible devotion she watched with deep disapproval; though she was not at all certain that her "young lady" was favorably disposed toward him. She could see and judge the feelings of the men, these many men who ate and drank and laughed and paid court to both the girls. Dr. Hale's brusque coldness she accepted, as from a higher order of being. Susie's gay coquetries were transparent to her; but Vivian she could not read so well.

The girl's deep conscientiousness, her courtesy and patience with all, and the gentle way in which she evaded the attentions so persistently offered, were new to Jeanne's experience. When Morton hung about and tried always to talk with Vivian exclusively, she saw her listen with kind attention, but somehow without any of that answering gleam which made Susie's blue eyes so irresistible.

"She has the lovers, but she has *no* beauty—to compare with my young lady!" Jeanne commented inwardly.

If the sad-eyed Jeanne had been of Scotch extraction instead of French, she might have quoted the explanation of the homely widow of three husbands when questioned by the good-looking spinster, who closed her inquiry by saying aggrievedly, "And ye'r na sae bonny."

"It's na the bonny that does it," explained the triple widow, "It's the come hither i' the een."

Susie's eyes sparkled with the "come hither," but those who came failed to make any marked progress. She was somewhat more cautious after the sudden approach and overthrow of Mr. A. Smith; yet more than one young gentleman boarder found business called him elsewhere, with marked suddenness; his place eagerly taken by another. The Cottonwoods had a waiting list, now.

Vivian made friends first, lovers afterward. Then if the love proved vain, the friendship had a way of lingering. Hers was one of those involved and over-conscientious characters, keenly sensitive to the thought of duty and to others' pain. She could not play with hearts that might be hurt in the handling, nor could she find in herself a quick and simple response to the appeals made to her; there were so many things to be considered.

Morton studied her with more intensity than he had ever before devoted to another human being; his admiration and respect grew with acquaintance, and all that was best in him rose in response to her wise, sweet womanliness. He had the background of their childhood's common experiences and her early sentiment—how much he did not know, to aid him. Then there was the unknown country of his years of changeful travel, many tales that he could tell her, many more which he found he could not.

He pressed his advantage, cautiously, finding the fullest response when he used the appeal to her uplifting influence. When they talked in the dining-room the sombre eye at the peephole watched with growing disapproval. The kitchen was largely left to her and her son by her fellow workers, on account of their nervous dislike for Theophile, and she utilized her opportunities.

Vivian had provided the boy with some big bright picture blocks, and he spent happy hours in matching them on the white scoured table, while his mother sewed, and watched. He had forgotten his burn by now, and she sewed contentedly for there was no one talking to her young lady but Dr. Hale, who lingered unaccountably.

To be sure, Vivian had brought him a plate of cakes from the pantry, and he seemed to find the little brown things efficiently seductive, or perhaps it was Grandma who held him, sitting bolt upright in her usual place, at the head of one table, and asking a series of firm but friendly questions. This she found the only way of inducing Dr. Hale to talk at all.

Yes, he was going away—Yes, he would be gone some time—A matter of weeks, perhaps—He could not say—His boys were all well—He did not wonder that they saw a good deal of them—It was a good place for them to come.

"You might come oftener yourself," said Grandma, "and play real whist with me. These young people play *Bridge!*" She used this word with angry scorn, as symbol of all degeneracy; and also despised pinochle, refusing to learn it, though any one could induce her to play bezique. Some of the more venturous and argumentative, strove to persuade her that the games were really the same.

"You needn't tell me," Mrs. Pettigrew would say, "I don't want to play any of your foreign games."

"But, Madam, bezique is not an English word," Professor Toomey had insisted, on one occasion; to which she had promptly responded, "Neither is 'bouquet!' "

Dr. Hale shook his head with a smile. He had a very nice smile, even Vivian admitted that. All the hard lines of his face curved and melted, and the light came into those deep-set eyes and shone warmly.

"I should enjoy playing whist with you very often, Mrs. Pettigrew; but a doctor has no time to call his own. And a good game of whist must not be interrupted by telephones."

"There's Miss Orella!" said Grandma, as the front door was heard to open. "She's getting to be quite a gadder."

"It does her good, I don't doubt," the doctor gravely remarked, rising to go. Miss Orella met him in the hall, and bade him good-bye with regret. "We do not see much of you, doctor; I hope you'll be back soon."

"Why it's only a little trip; you good people act as if I were going to Alaska," he said, "It makes me feel as if I had a family!"

"Pity you haven't," remarked Grandma with her usual definiteness. Dykeman stood holding Miss Orella's wrap, with his dry smile. "Good-bye, Hale," he said. "I'll chaperon your orphan asylum for you. So long."

"Come out into the dining-room," said Miss Orella, after Dr. Hale had departed. "I know you must be hungry," and Mr. Dykeman did not deny it. In his quiet middle-aged way, he enjoyed this enlarged family circle as much as the younger fellows, and he and Mr. Unwin seemed to vie with one another to convince Miss Orella that life still held charms for her. Mr. Skee also hovered about her to a considerable extent, but most of his devotion was bestowed upon damsels of extreme youth.

"Here's one that's hungry, anyhow," remarked Dr. Bellair, coming out of her office at the moment, with her usual clean and clear-starched appearance. "I've been at it for eighteen hours, with only bites to eat. Yes, all over; both doing well."

It was a source of deep self-congratulation to Dr. Bellair to watch her friend grow young again in the new atmosphere. To Susie it appeared somewhat preposterous, as her Aunt seems to her mind a permanently elderly person; while to Mrs. Pettigrew it looked only natural. "Rella's only a young thing anyway," was her comment. But Jane Bellair marked and approved the added grace of each new gown, the blossoming of lace and ribbon, the appearance of long-hoarded bits of family jewelry, things held "too showy to wear" in Bainville, but somehow quite appropriate here.

Vivian and Grandma made Miss Orella sit down at her own table head, and bustled about in the pantry, bringing cheese and crackers, cake and fruit; but the doctor poked her head through the swing door and demanded meat.

"I don't want a refection, I want food," she said, and Jeanne cheerfully brought her a plate of cold beef. She was much attached to Dr. Bellair, for reasons many and good.

"What I like about this place," said Mrs. Pettigrew, surveying the scene from the head of her table, "is that there's always something going on."

"What I like about it," remarked Dr. Bellair, between well-Fletcherized mouthfuls, "is that people have a chance to grow and are growing."

"What I like," Mr. Dykeman looked about him, and paused in the middle of a sentence, as was his wont; "is being beautifully taken care of and made comfortable—any man likes that."

Miss Orella beamed upon him. Emboldened, he went on: "And what I like most is the new, delightful"—he was gazing admiringly at her, and she looked so embarrassed that he concluded with a wide margin of safety—"friends I'm making."

Miss Orella's rosy flush, which had risen under his steady gaze, ebbed again to her usual soft pink. Even her coldest critics, in the most caustic Bainvillian circles, could never deny that she had "a good complexion." New England, like old England, loves roses on the cheeks, and our dry Western winds play havoc with them. But Miss Orella's bloomed brighter than at home.

"It is pleasant," she said softly; "all this coming and going—and the nice people—who stay." She looked at no one in particular, yet Mr. Dykeman seemed pleased.

"There's another coming, I guess," remarked Grandma, as a carriage was heard to stop outside, the gate slammed, and trunk-burdened steps pounded heavily across the piazza. The bell rang sharply, Mr. Dykeman opened the door, and the trunk came in first—a huge one, dumped promptly on the hall floor.

Behind the trunk and the man beneath it entered a lady; slim, elegant, graceful, in a rich silk dust coat and soft floating veils.

"Mr. dear Miss Elder!" she said, coming forward; "and Vivian! Dear Vivian! I thought you could put me up, somewhere, and told him to come right here. O—and please—I haven't a bit of change left in my purse—will you pay the man?"

"Well, if it isn't Mrs. St. Cloud," said Grandma, without any note of welcome in her voice.

Mr. Dykeman paid the man; looked at the trunk, and paid him some more. The man departed swearing softly at nothing in particular, and Mr. Dykeman departed also to his own room.

Miss Orella's hospitable soul was much exercised. Refuse shelter to an old acquaintance, a guest, however unexpected, she could not; yet she had no vacant room. Vivian, flushed and excited, moved anew by her old attraction, eagerly helped the visitor take off her wraps, Mrs. Pettigrew standing the while, with her arms folded, in the doorway of her room, her thin lips drawn to a hard line, as one intending to repel boarders at any risk to life or limb. Dr. Bellair had returned to her apartments at the first sound of the visitor's voice.

She, gracious and calm in the midst of confusion, sat in a wreath of downdropped silken wrappings, and held Vivian's hand.

"You dear child!" she said, "how well you look! What a charming place this is. The doctors sent me West for my health; I'm on my way to California. But when I found the train stopped here—I didn't know that it did till I saw the name—I had them take my trunk right off, and here I am! It is such a pleasure to see you all."

"Huh!" said Mrs. Pettigrew, and disappeared completely, closing the door behind her.

"Anything will do, Miss Elder," the visitor went on. "I shall find a hall bedroom palatial after a sleeping car; or a garret—anything! It's only for a few days, you know."

Vivian was restraining herself from hospitable offers by remembering that her room was also Susie's, and Miss Orella well knew that to give up hers meant sleeping on a hard, short sofa in that all-too-public parlor. She was hastily planning in her mind to take Susie in with her and persuade Mrs. Pettigrew to harbor Vivian, somewhat deterred by memories of the old lady's expression as she departed, when Mr. Dykeman appeared at the door, suitcase in hand.

"I promised Hale I'd keep house for those fatherless boys, you know," he said. "In the meantime, you're quite welcome to use my room, Miss Elder." And he departed, her blessing going with him.

More light refreshments were now in order, Mrs. St. Cloud protesting that she wanted nothing, but finding much to praise in the delicacies set before her. Several of the other boarders drifted in, always glad of an extra bite before going to bed. Susie and Mr. Saunders returned from a walk, Morton reappeared, and Jeanne, peering sharply in, resentful of this new drain upon her pantry shelves, saw a fair, sweet-faced woman, seated at ease, eating daintily, while Miss Elder and Vivian waited upon her, and the men all gathered admiringly about. Jeanne Jeaune wagged her head. "Ah, ha, Madame!" she muttered softly, "Such as you I have met before!" Theophile she had long since sent to bed, remaining up herself to keep an eye on the continued disturbance in the front of the house. Vivian and Susie brought the dishes out, and would have washed them or left them till morning for the maids.

"Truly, no," said Jeanne Jeaune; "go you to your beds; I will attend to these."

One by one she heard them go upstairs, distant movement and soft dissuasion as two gentlemen insisted on bearing Mrs. St. Cloud's trunk into her room, receding voices and closing doors. There was no sound in the dining-room now, but still she waited; the night was not yet quiet.

Miss Elder and Susie, Vivian also, hovered about, trying to make this new guest comfortable, in spite of her graceful protests that they must not concern themselves in the least about her, that she wanted nothing—absolutely nothing. At last they left her, and still later, after some brief exchange of surprised comment and warm appreciation of Mr. Dykeman's thoughtfulness, the family retired. Vivian, when her long hair was smoothly braided for the night, felt an imperative need for water.

"Don't you want some, Susie? I'll bring you a glass." But Susie only huddled the bedclothes about her pretty shoulders and said:

"Don't bring me *anything,* until to-morrow morning!"

So her room-mate stole out softly in her wrapper, remembering that a pitcher of cool water still stood on one of the tables. The windows to the street let in a flood of light from a big street lamp, and she found her way easily, but was a bit startled for a moment to find a man still sitting there, his head upon his arms.

"Why, Morton," she said; "is that you? What are you sitting up for? It's awfully late. I'm just after some water." She poured a glassful. "Don't you want some?"

"No, thank you," he said. "Yes, I will. Give me some, please."

The girl gave him a glass, drank from her own and set it down, turning to go, but he reached out and caught a flowing sleeve of her kimono.

"Don't go, Vivian! Do sit down and talk to a fellow. I've been trying to see you for days and days."

"Why, Morton Elder, how absurd! You have certainly seen me every day, and we've talked hours this very evening. This is no time for conversation, surely."

"The best time in the world," he assured her. "All the other times there are people about—dozens—hundreds—swarms! I want to talk to just you."

There were certainly no dozens or hundreds about now, but as certainly there was one, noting with keen and disapproving interest this midnight tête-à-tête. It did not last very long, and was harmless and impersonal enough while it lasted.

Vivian sat for a few moments, listening patiently while the young man talked of his discouragements, his hopes, his wishes to succeed in life, to be worthy of her; but when the personal note sounded, when he tried to take her hand in the semi-darkness, then her New England conscience sounded also, and she rose to her feet and left him.

"We'll talk about that another time," she said. "Now do be quiet and do not wake people up."

He stole upstairs, dutifully, and she crept softly back to her room and got into bed, without eliciting more than a mild grunt from sleepy Susie. Silence reigned at last in the house. Not for long, however.

At about half past twelve Dr. Bellair was roused from a well-earned sleep by a light, insistent tap upon her door. She listened, believing it to be a wind-stirred twig; but no, it was a finger tap—quiet—repeated. She opened the door upon Jeanne in her stocking feet.

"Your pardon, Mrs. Doctor," said the visitor, "but it is of importance. May I speak for a little? No, I'm not ill, and we need not a light."

They sat in the clean little office, the swaying cottonwood boughs making a changeful pattern on the floor.

"You are a doctor, and you can make an end to it—you must make an end to it," said Jeanne, after a little hesitation. "This young man—this nephew—he must not marry my young lady."

"What makes you think he wants to?" asked the doctor.

"I have seen, I have heard—I know," said Jeanne. "You know, all can see that he loves her. *He!* Not such as he for my young lady."

"Why do you object to him, Jeanne?"

"He has lived the bad life," said the woman, grimly.

"Most young men are open to criticism," said Dr. Bellair. "Have you anything definite to tell me—anything that you could *prove?*—if it were necessary to save her?" She leaned forward, elbows on knees.

Jeanne sat in the flickering shadows, considering her words. "He has had the sickness," she said at last.

"Can you prove that?"

"I can prove to you, a doctor, that Coralie and Anastasia and Estelle—they have had it. They are still alive; but not so beautiful."

"Yes; but how can you prove it on him?"

"I know he was with them. Well, it was no secret. I myself have seen—he was there often."

"How on earth have you managed not to be recognized?" Dr. Bellair inquired after a few moments.

Jeanne laughed bitterly. "That was eight years ago; he was but a boy—gay and foolish, with the others. What does a boy know? . . . Also, at that time I was blonde, and—of a difference."

"I see," said the doctor, "I see! That's pretty straight. You know personally of that time, and you know the record of those others. But that was a long time ago."

"I have heard of him since, many times, in such company," said Jeanne. They sat in silence for some time. A distant church clock struck a single deep low note. The woman rose, stood for a hushed moment, suddenly burst forth with hushed intensity: "You must save her, doctor—you will! I was young once," she went on. "I did not know—as she does not. I married, and—*that* came to me! It made me a devil—for awhile. Tell her, doctor—if you must; tell her about my boy!"

She went away, weeping silently, and Dr. Bellair sat sternly thinking in her chair, and fell asleep in it from utter weariness.

8

A MIXTURE

In poetry and painting and fiction we see
  Such praise for the Dawn of the Day,
We've long since been convinced that a sunrise must be
  All Glorious and Golden and Gay.

But we find there are mornings quite foggy and drear,
  With the clouds in a low-hanging pall;
Till the grey light of daylight can hardly make clear
  That the sun has arisen at all.

Dr. Richard Hale left his brood of temporary orphans without really expecting for them any particular oversight from Andrew Dykeman; but the two were sufficiently close friends to well warrant the latter in moving over to The Monastery—as Jimmie Saunders called it.

Mr. Dykeman was sufficiently popular with the young men to be welcome, even if he had not had a good excuse, and when they found how super-excellent his excuse was they wholly approved.

To accommodate Miss Orella was something—all the boys liked Miss Orella. They speculated among themselves on her increasing youth and good looks, and even exchanged sagacious theories as to the particular acting cause. But when they found that Mr. Dykeman's visit was to make room for the installation of Mrs. St. Cloud, they were more than pleased.

All the unexpressed ideals of masculine youth seemed centered in this palely graceful lady; the low, sweet voice, the delicate hands, the subtle sympathy of manner, the nameless, quiet charm of dress.

Young Burns became her slave on sight, Lawson and Peters fell on the second day; not one held out beyond the third. Even Susie's attractions paled, her very youth became a disadvantage; she lacked that large considering tenderness.

"Fact is," Mr. Peters informed his friends rather suddenly, "young women are selfish. Naturally, of course. It takes some experience to—well, to understand a fellow." They all agreed with him.

Mr. Dykeman, quiet and reserved as always, was gravely polite to the newcomer, and Mr. Skee revolved at a distance, making observations. Occasionally he paid some court to her, at which times she was cold to him; and again he devoted himself to the other ladies with his impressive air, as of one bowing low and sweeping the floor with a plumed hat.

Mr. Skee's Stetson had, as a matter of fact, no sign of plumage, and his bows were of a somewhat jerky order; but his gallantry was sweeping and impressive, none the less. If he remained too far away Mrs. St. Cloud would draw him to her circle, which consisted of all the other gentlemen.

There were two exceptions. Mr. James Saunders had reached the stage where any woman besides Susie was but a skirted ghost, and Morton was by this time so deeply devoted to Vivian that he probably would not have wavered even if left alone. He was not wholly a free agent, however.

Adela St. Cloud had reached an age when something must be done. Her mysterious absent husband had mysteriously and absently died, and still she never breathed a word against him. But the Bible Class in Bainville furnished no satisfactory material for further hopes, the place of her earlier dwelling seemed not wholly desirable now, and the West had called her.

Finding herself comfortably placed in Mr. Dykeman's room, and judging from the number of his shoe-trees and the quality of his remaining toilet articles that he might be considered "suitable," she decided to remain in the half-way house for a season. So settled, why, for a thousand reasons one must keep one's hand in.

There were men in plenty, from twenty year old Archie to the uncertain decades of Mr. Skee. Idly amusing herself, she questioned that gentleman indirectly as to his age, drawing from him astounding memories of the previous century.

When confronted with historic proof that the events he described were over a hundred years passed, he would apologize, admitting that he had no memory for dates. She owned one day, with gentle candor, to being thirty-three.

"That must seem quite old to a man like you, Mr. Skee. I feel very old sometimes!" She lifted large eyes to him, and drew her filmy scarf around her shoulders.

"Your memory must be worse than mine, ma'am," he replied, "and work the same way. You've sure got ten or twenty years added on superfluous! Now me!" He shook his head; "I don't remember when I was born at all. And losin' my folks so young, *and* the family Bible—I don't expect I ever shall. But I 'low I'm all of ninety-seven."

This being palpably impossible, and as the only local incidents he could recall in his youth were quite dateless adventures among the Indians, she gave it up. Why Mr. Skee should have interested her at all was difficult to say, unless it was the appeal to his uncertainty—he was at least a game fish, if not edible.

Of the women she met, Susie and Vivian were far the most attractive, wherefore Mrs. St. Cloud, with subtle sympathy and engaging frankness, fairly cast Mr. Saunders in Susie's arms, and vice versa, as opportunity occurred.

Morton she rather snubbed, treated him as a mere boy, told tales of his childhood that were in no way complimentary—so that he fled from her.

With Vivian she renewed her earlier influence to a great degree.

With some inquiry and more intuition she discovered what it was that had chilled the girl's affection for her.

"I don't wonder, my dear child," she said; "I never told you of that—I never speak of it to anyone. . . . It was one of the—" she shivered slightly—"darkest griefs of a very dark time. . . . He was a beautiful boy. . . . I never *dreamed*—"

The slow tears rose in her beautiful eyes till they shone like shimmering stars.

"Heaven send no such tragedy may ever come into your life, dear!"

She reached a tender hand to clasp the girl's. "I am so glad of your happiness!"

Vivian was silent. As a matter of fact, she was not happy enough to honestly accept sympathy. Mrs. St. Cloud mistook her attitude, or seemed to.

"I suppose you still blame me. Many people did. I often blame myself. One cannot be *too* careful. It's a terrible responsibility, Vivian—to have a man love you."

The girl's face grew even more somber. That was one thing which was troubling her.

"But your life is all before you," pursued the older woman. "Your dream has come true! How happy—how wonderfully happy you must be!"

"I am not, not *really,*" said the girl. "At least—"

"I know—I know; I understand," Mrs. St. Cloud nodded with tender wisdom. "You are not sure. Is not that it?"

That was distinctly "it," and Vivian so agreed.

"There is no other man?"

"Not the shadow of one!" said the girl firmly. And as her questioner had studied the field and made up her mind to the same end, she believed her.

"Then you must not mind this sense of uncertainty. It always happens. It is part of the morning clouds of maidenhood, my dear—it vanishes with the sunrise!" And she smiled beatifically.

Then the girl unburdened herself of her perplexities. She could always express herself so easily to this sympathetic friend.

"There are so many things that I—dislike—about him," she said. "Habits of speech—of manners. He is not—not what I—"

She paused.

"Not all the Dream! Ah! My dear child, they never are! We are given these beautiful ideals to guard and guide us; but the real is never quite the same. But when a man's soul opens to you—when he loves—these small things vanish. They can be changed—you will change them."

"Yes—he says so," Vivian admitted. "He says that he knows that he is—unworthy—and has done wrong things. But so have I, for that matter."

Mrs. St. Cloud agreed with her. "I am glad you feel that, my dear. Men have their temptations—their vices—and we good women are apt to be hard on them. But have we no faults? Ah, my dear, I have seen good women—young girls, like yourself—ruin a man's whole life by—well, by heartlessness; by lack of understanding. Most young men do things they become ashamed of when they really love. And in the case of a motherless boy like this—lonely, away from his home, no good woman's influence about—what else could we expect? But you can make a new man of him. A glorious work!"

"That's what he says. I'm not so sure—" The girl hesitated.

"Not sure you can? Oh, my child, it is the most beautiful work on earth! To see from year to year a strong, noble character grow under your helping hand! To be the guiding star, the inspiration of a man's life. To live to hear him say:

"'Ah, who am I that God should bow
  From heaven to choose a wife for me?
What have I done He should endow
  My home with thee?'"

There was a silence.

Vivian's dark eyes shone with appreciation for the tender beauty of the lines, the lovely thought. Then she arose and walked nervously across the floor, returning presently.

"Mrs. St. Cloud—"

"Call me Adela, my dear."

"Adela—dear Adela—you—you have been married. I have no mother. Tell me, ought not there to be more—more love? I'm fond of Morton, of course, and I do want to help him—but surely, if I loved him—I should feel happier—more sure!"

"The first part of love is often very confusing, my dear. I'll tell you how it is: just because you are a woman grown and feel your responsibilities, especially here, where you have so many men friends, you keep Morton at a distance. Then the external sort of cousinly affection you have for him rather blinds you to other feelings. But I have not forgotten—and I'm sure you have not—the memory of that hot, sweet night so long ago; the world swimming in summer moonlight and syringa sweetness; the stillness everywhere—and your first kiss!"

Vivian started to her feet. She moved to the window and stood awhile; came back and kissed her friend warmly, and went away without another word.

The lady betook herself to her toilet, and spent some time on it, for there was one of Miss Peeder's classes that night.

Mrs. St. Cloud danced with many, but most with Mr. Dykeman; no woman in the room had her swimming grace of motion, and yet, with all the throng of partners about her she had time to see Susie's bright head bobbing about beneath Mr. Saunders downbent, happy face, and Vivian, with her eyes cast down, dancing with Morton, whose gaze never left her. He was attention itself, he brought her precisely the supper she liked, found her favorite corner to rest in, took her to sit on the broad piazza between dances, remained close to her, still talking earnestly, when all the outsiders had gone.

Vivian found it hard to sleep that night. All that he had said of his new hope, new power, new courage, bore out Mrs. St. Cloud's bright promise of a new-built life. And some way, as she had listened and did not forbid, the touch of his hand, the pressure of his arm, grew warmer and brought back the memories of that summer night so long ago.

He had begged hard for a kiss before he left her, and she quite had to tear herself away, as Susie drifted in, also late; and Aunt Orella said they must all go to bed right away—she was tired if they were not.

She did look tired. This dance seemed somehow less agreeable to her than had others. She took off her new prettinesses and packed them away in a box in the lower drawer.

"I'm an old fool!" she said. "Trying to dress up like a girl. I'm ashamed of myself!" Quite possibly she did not sleep well either, yet she had no room-mate to keep her awake by babbling on, as Susie did to Vivian.

Her discourse was first, last and always about Jimmie Saunders. He had said this, he had looked that, he had done so; and what did Vivian think he meant? And wasn't he handsome—and *so* clever!

Little Susie cuddled close and finally dropped off asleep, her arms around Vivian. But the older girl counted the hours; her head, or her heart, in a whirl.

Morton Elder was wakeful, too. So much so that he arose with a whispered expletive, took his shoes in his hand, and let himself softly out for a tramp in the open.

This was not the first of his love affairs, but with all his hot young heart he wished it was. He stood still, alone on the high stretches of moonlit mesa and looked up at the measureless, brilliant spaces above him.

"I'll keep straight—if I can have her!" he repeated under his breath. "I will! I will!"

It had never occurred to him before to be ashamed of the various escapades of his youth. He had done no more than others, many others. None of "the boys" he associated with intended to do what was wrong; they were quite harsh in judgment of those who did, according to their standards. None of them had been made acquainted with the social or pathological results of their amusements, and the mere "Zutritt ist Verboten" had never impressed them at all.

But now the gentler influences of his childhood, even the narrow morality of Bainville, rose in pleasant colors in his mind. He wished he had saved his money, instead of spending it faster than it came in. He wished he had kept out of poker and solo and barrooms generally. He wished, in a dumb, shamed way, that he could come to her as clean as she was. But he threw his shoulders back and lifted his head determinedly.

"I'll be good to her," he determined; "I'll make her a good husband."

In the days that followed his devotion was as constant as before, but more intelligent. His whole manner changed and softened. He began to read the books she liked, and to talk about them. He was gentler to everyone, more polite, even to the waitresses, tender and thoughtful of his aunt and sister. Vivian began to feel a pride in him, and in her influence, deepening as time passed.

Mrs. Pettigrew, visiting the library on one of her frequent errands, was encountered there and devotedly escorted home by Mr. Skee.

"That is a most fascinating young lady who has Mr. Dykeman's room; don't you think so, ma'am?" quoth he.

"I do not," said Mrs. Pettigrew. "Young! She's not so young as you are—nothing like—never was!"

He threw back his head and laughed his queer laugh, which looked so uproarious and made so little noise.

"She certainly is a charmer, whatever her age may be," he continued.

"Glad you think so, Mr. Skee. It may be time you lost a fourth!"

"Lost a fourth? What in the—Hesperides!"

"If you can't guess what, you needn't ask me!" said the lady, with some tartness. "But for my own part I prefer the Apaches. Good afternoon, Mr. Skee."

She betook herself to her room with unusual promptness, and refused to be baited forth by any kind of offered amusement.

"It's right thoughtful of Andy Dykeman, gettin' up this entertainment for Mrs. St. Cloud, isn't it, Mrs. Elder?" Thus Mr. Skee to Miss Orella a little later.

"I don't think it is Mr. Dykeman's idea at all," she told him. "It's those boys over there. They are all wild about her, quite naturally." She gave a little short sigh. "If Dr. Hale were at home I doubt if he would encourage it."

"I'm pretty sure he wouldn't, Ma'am. He's certainly down on the fair sex, even such a peacherino as this one. But with Andy, now, it's different. He is a man of excellent judgment."

"I guess all men's judgment is pretty much alike in some ways," said Miss Orella, oracularly. She seemed busy and constrained, and Mr. Skee drifted off and paid court as best he might to Dr. Bellair.

"Charmed to find you at home, Ma'am," he said; "or shall I say at office?"

"Call it what you like, Mr. Skee; it's been my home for a good many years now."

"It's a mighty fine thing for a woman, livin' alone, to have a business, seems to me," remarked the visitor.

"It's a fine thing for any woman, married or single, to my mind," she answered. "I wish I could get Vivian Lane started in that kindergarten she talks about."

"There's kids enough, and goodness knows they need a gardener! What's lackin'? House room?"

"She thinks she's not really competent. She has no regular certificate, you see. Her parents would never let go of her long enough," the doctor explained.

"Some parents *are* pretty graspin', ain't they? To my mind, Miss Vivian would be a better teacher than lots of the ticketed ones. She's got the natural love of children."

"Yes, and she has studied a great deal. She just needs an impetus."

"Perhaps if she thought there was 'a call' she might be willing. I doubt if the families here realize what they're missin'. Aint there some among your patients who could be stirred up a little?"

The doctor thought there were, and he suggested several names from his apparently unlimited acquaintance.

"I believe in occupation for the young. It takes up their minds," said Mr. Skee, and departed with serenity. He strolled over to Dr. Hale's fence and leaned upon it, watching the preparations. Mr. Dykeman, in his shirt-sleeves, stood about offering suggestions, while the young men swarmed here and there with poles and stepladders, hanging Chinese lanterns.

"Hello, Elmer; come in and make yourself useful," called Mr. Dykeman.

"I'll come in, but I'll be switched if I'll be useful," he replied, laying a large hand on the fence and vaulting his long legs over it with an agility amazing in one of his alleged years. "You are all sure putting yourself out for this occasion. Is it somebody's birthday?"

"No; it's a get-up of these youngsters. They began by wanting Mrs. St. Cloud to come over to tea—afternoon tea—and now look at this!"

"Did she misunderstand the invitation as bad as that?"

"O, no; just a gradual change of plan. One thing leads to another, you know. Here, Archie! That bush won't hold the line. Put it on the willow."

"I see," said Mr. Skee; "and, as we're quotin' proverbs, I might remark that 'While the cat's away the mice will play.'"

Mr. Dykeman smiled. "It's rather a good joke on Hale, isn't it?"

"Would be if he should happen to come home—and find this hen-party on." They both chuckled.

"I guess he's good for a week yet," said Mr. Dykeman. "Those medical associations do a lot of talking. Higher up there, George—a good deal higher."

He ran over to direct the boys, and Mr. Skee, hands behind him, strolled up and down the garden, wearing a meditative smile. He and Andrew Dykeman had been friends for many long years.

Dr. Bellair used her telephone freely after Mr. Skee's departure, making notes and lists of names. Late in the afternoon she found Vivian in the hall.

"I don't see much of you these days, Miss Lane," she said.

The girl flushed. Since Mrs. St. Cloud's coming and their renewed intimacy she had rather avoided the doctor, and that lady had kept herself conspicuously out of the way.

"Don't call me Miss Lane; I'm Vivian—to my friends."

"I hope you count me a friend?" said Dr. Bellair, gravely.

"I do, Doctor, and I'm proud to. But so many things have been happening lately," she laughed, a little nervously. "The truth is, I'm really ashamed to talk to you; I'm so lazy."

"That's exactly what I wanted to speak about. Aren't you ready to begin that little school of yours?"

"I'd like to—I should, really," said the girl. "But, somehow, I don't know how to set about it."

"I've been making some inquiries," said the doctor. "There are six or eight among my patients that you could count on—about a dozen young ones. How many could you handle?"

"Oh, I oughtn't to have more than twenty in any case. A dozen would be plenty to begin with. Do you think I *could* count on them—really?"

"I tell you what I'll do," her friend offered; "I'll take you around and introduce you to any of them you don't know. Most of 'em come here to the dances. There's Mrs. Horsford and Mrs. Blake, and that little Mary Jackson with the twins. You'll find they are mostly friends."

"You are awfully kind," said the girl. "I wish"—her voice took on a sudden note of intensity—"I do wish I were strong, like you, Dr. Bellair."

"I wasn't very strong—at your age—my child. I did the weakest of weak things—"

Vivian was eager to ask her what it was, but a door opened down one side passage and the doctor quietly disappeared down the other, as Mrs. St. Cloud came out.

"I though I heard your voice," she said. "And Miss Elder's, wasn't it?"

"No; it was Dr. Bellair."

"A strong character, and a fine physician, I understand. I'm sorry she does not like me."

Mrs. St. Cloud's smile made it seem impossible that anyone should dislike her.

Vivian could not, however, deny the fact, and was not diplomatic enough to smooth it over, which her more experienced friend proceeded to do.

"It is temperamental," she said gently. "If we had gone to school together we would not have been friends. She is strong, downright, progressive; I am weaker, more sensitive, better able to bear than to do. You must find her so stimulating."

"Yes," the girl said. "She was talking to me about my school."

"Your school?"

"Didn't you know I meant to have a sort of kindergarten? We planned it even before starting; but Miss Elder seemed to need me at first, and since then—things—have happened—"

"And other things will happen, dear child! Quite other and different things."

The lady's smile was bewitching. Vivian flushed slowly under her gaze.

"Oh, my dear, I watched you dancing together! You don't mind my noticing, do you?"

Her voice was suddenly tender and respectful. "I do not wish to intrude, but you are very dear to me. Come into my room—do—and tell me what to wear to-night."

Mrs. St. Cloud's clothes had always been a delight to Vivian. They were what she would have liked to wear—and never quite have dared, under the New England fear of being "too dressy." Her own beauty was kept trimly neat, like a closed gentian.

Her friend was in the gayest mood. She showed her a trunkful of delicate garments and gave her a glittering embroidered scarf, which the girl rapturously admired, but declared she would never have the courage to wear.

"You shall wear it this very night," declared the lady. "Here—show me what you've got. You shall be as lovely as you *are,* for once!"

So Vivian brought out her modest wardrobe, and the older woman chose a gown of white, insisted on shortening the sleeves to fairy wings of lace, draped the scarf about her white neck, raised the soft, close-bound hair to a regal crown, and put a shining star in it, and added a string of pearls on the white throat.

"Look at yourself now, child!" she said.

Vivian looked, in the long depths of Mr. Dykeman's mirror. She knew that she had beauty, but had never seen herself so brilliantly attired. Erect, slender, graceful, the long lines of her young body draped in soft white, and her dark head, crowned and shining, poised on its white column, rising from the shimmering lace. Her color deepened as she looked, and added to the picture.

"You shall wear it to-night! You shall!" cried her admiring friend. "To please me—if no one else!"

Whether to please her or someone else, Vivian consented, the two arriving rather late at the garden party across the way.

Mr. Dykeman, looking very tall and fine in his evening clothes, was a cordial host, ably seconded by the eager boys about him.

The place was certainly a credit to their efforts, the bare rooms being turned to bowers by vines and branches brought from the mountains, and made fragrant by piled flowers. Lights glimmered through colored shades among the leaves, and on the dining table young Peters, who came from Connecticut, had rigged a fountain by means of some rubber tubing and an auger hole in the floor. This he had made before Mr. Dykeman caught him, and vowed Dr. Hale would not mind. Mr. Peters' enjoyment of the evening, however, was a little dampened by his knowledge of the precarious nature of this arrangement. He danced attendance on Mrs. St. Cloud, with the others, but wore a preoccupied expression, and stole in once or twice from the lit paths outside to make sure that all was running well. It was well to and during supper time, and the young man was complimented on his ingenuity.

"Reminds me of the Hanging Gardens of Babylon," said Mr. Skee, sentimentally.

"Why?" asked Mrs. Pettigrew.

"Oh, *why,* Ma'am? How can a fellow say why?" he protested. "Because it is so—so efflorescent, I suppose."

"Reminds me of a loose faucet," said she, *sotto voce,* to Dr. Bellair.

Mr. Peters beamed triumphantly, but in the very hour of his glory young Burns, hastening to get a cup of coffee for his fair one, tripped over the concealed pipe, and the fountain poured forth its contributions among the feet of the guests.

This was a minor misadventure, however, hurting no one's feeling but Mr. Peters', and Mrs. St. Cloud was so kind to him in consequence that he was envied by all the others.

Mr. Dykeman was attentive to his guests, old and young, but Mrs. Pettigrew had not her usual smile for him; Miss Orella declined to dance, alleging that she was too tired, and Dr. Bellair somewhat drily told him that he need not bother with her. He was hardly to be blamed if he turned repeatedly to Mrs. St. Cloud, whose tactful sweetness was always ready. She had her swarm of young admirers about her, yet never failed to find a place for her host, a smile and a word of understanding.

Her eyes were everywhere. She watched Mr. Skee waltzing with the youngest, providing well-chosen refreshments for Miss Orella, gallantly escorting Grandma to see the "Lovers' Lane" they had made at the end of the garden. Its twin lines of lights were all outside; within was grateful shadow.

Mrs. St. Cloud paced through this fragrant arbor with each and every one of the receiving party, uttering ever-fresh expressions of admiration and gratitude for their kind thoughtfulness, especially to Mr. Dykeman.

When she saw Susie and Mr. Saunders go in at the farther end, she constituted herself a sort of protective agency to keep every one else out, holding them in play with various pleasant arts.

And Vivian? When she arrived there was a little gasp from Morton, who was waiting for her near the door. She was indeed a sight to make a lover's heart leap. He had then, as it were, surrounded her. Vainly did the others ask for dances. Morton had unblushingly filled out a card with his own name and substituted it for the one she handed him. She protested, but the music sounded and he whirled her away before she could expostulate to any avail.

His eyes spoke his admiration, and for once his tongue did not spoil the impression.

Half laughing and half serious, she let him monopolize her, but quite drove him away when Mr. Dykeman claimed his dance.

"All filled up!" said Morton for her, showing his card.

"Mine was promised yesterday, was it not, Miss Lane?" said the big man, smiling. And she went with him. He took her about the garden later, gravely admiring and attentive, and when Susie fairly rushed into her arms, begging her to come and talk with her, he left them both in a small rose-crowned summer-house and went back to Mrs. St. Cloud.

"Oh, Vivian, Vivian! What do you think!" Susie's face was buried on Vivian's shoulder. "I'm engaged!"

Vivian held her close and kissed her soft hair. Her joyous excitement was contagious.

"He's the nicest man in the world!" breathed Susie, "and he loves me!"

"We all supposed he did. Didn't you know it before?"

"Oh, yes, in a way; but, Vivian—he kissed me!"

"Well, child, have you never in all your little life been kissed before?"

Susie lifted a rosy, tearful face for a moment.

"Never, never, never!" she said. "I thought I had, but I haven't! Oh, I am so happy!"

"What's up?" inquired Morton, appearing with a pink lantern in his hand, in impatient search for his adored one. "Susie—crying?"

"No, I'm *not,*" she said, and ran forthwith back to the house, whence Jimmy was bringing her ice cream.

Vivian started to follow her.

"Oh, no, Vivian; don't go. Wait." He dropped the lantern and took her hands. The paper cover flared up, showing her flushed cheeks and starry eyes. He stamped out the flame, and in the sudden darkness caught her in his arms.

For a moment she allowed him, turning her head away. He kissed her white shoulder.

"No! No, Morton—don't! You mustn't!"

She tried to withdraw herself, but he held her fast. She could feel the pounding of his heart.

"Oh, Vivian, don't say no! You will marry me, won't you? Some day, when I'm more worth while. Say you will! Some day—if not now. I love you so; I need you so! Say yes, Vivian."

He was breathing heavily. His arms held her motionless. She still kept her face turned from him.

"Let me go, Morton; let me go! You hurt me!"

"Say yes, dear, and I'll let you go—for a little while."

"Yes," said Vivian.

The ground jarred beside them, as a tall man jumped the hedge boundary. He stood a moment, staring.

"Well, is this my house, or Coney Island?" they heard him

say. And then Morton swore softly to himself as Vivian left him and came out.

"Good evening, Dr. Hale," she said, a little breathlessly. "We weren't expecting you so soon."

"I should judge not," he answered. "What's up, anyhow?"

"The boys—and Mr. Dykeman—are giving a garden party for Mrs. St. Cloud."

"For whom?"

"For Adela St. Cloud. She is visiting us. Aren't you coming in?"

"Not now," he said, and was gone without another word.

9

CONSEQUENCES

You may have a fondness for grapes that are green,
And the sourness that greenness beneath;
You may have a right
To a colic at night—
But consider your children's teeth!

Dr. Hale retired from his gaily illuminated grounds in too much displeasure to consider the question of dignity. One suddenly acting cause was the news given him by Vivian. The other was the sight of Morton Elder's face as he struck a match to light his cigarette.

Thus moved, and having entered and left his own grounds like a thief in the night, he proceeded to tramp in the high-lying outskirts of the town until every light in his house had gone out. Then he returned, let himself into his office, and lay there on a lounge until morning.

Vivian had come out so quickly to greet the doctor from obscure motives. She felt a sudden deep objection to being found there with Morton, a wish to appear as one walking about unconcernedly, and when that match glow made Morton's face shine out prominently in the dark shelter, she, too, felt a sudden displeasure.

Without a word she went swiftly to the house, excused herself to her Grandmother, who nodded understandingly, and returned to The Cottonwoods, to her room. She felt that she must be alone and think; think of that irrevocable word she had uttered, and its consequences.

She sat at her window, rather breathless, watching the rows of pink lanterns swaying softly on the other side of the street; hearing the lively music, seeing young couples leave the gate and stroll off homeward.

Susie's happiness came more vividly to mind than her own. It was so freshly joyous, so pure, so perfectly at rest. She could not feel that way, could not tell with decision exactly how she did feel. But if this was happiness, it was not as she had imagined it. She thought of that moonlit summer night so long ago, and the memory of its warm wonder seemed sweeter than the hasty tumult and compulsion of to-night.

She was stirred through and through by Morton's intense emotion, but with a sort of reaction, a wish to escape. He had been so madly anxious, he had held her so close; there seemed no other way but to yield to him—in order to get away.

And then Dr. Hale had jarred the whole situation. She had to be polite to him, in his own grounds. If only Morton had kept still—that grating match—his face, bent and puffing, Dr. Hale must have seen him. And again she thought of little Susie with almost envy. Even after that young lady had come in, bubbled over with confidences and raptures, and finally dropped to sleep without Vivian's having been able to bring herself to return the confidences, she stole back to her window again to breathe.

Why had Dr. Hale started so at the name of Mrs. St. Cloud? That was puzzling her more than she cared to admit. By and by she saw his well-known figure, tall and erect, march by on the other side and go into the office.

"O, well," she sighed at last, "I'm not young, like Susie. Perhaps it *is* like this—"

Now Morton had been in no special need of that cigarette at that special moment, but he did not wish to seem to hide in the dusky arbor, nor to emerge lamely as if he had hidden. So he lit the match, more from habit than anything else. When it was out, and the cigarette well lighted, he heard the doctor's sudden thump on the other side of the fence and came out to rejoin Vivian. She was not there.

He did not see her again that night, and his meditations were such that next day found him, as a lover, far more agreeable to Vivian than the night before. He showed real understanding, no triumph, no airs of possession; took no liberties, only said: "When I am good enough

I shall claim you—my darling!" and looked at her with such restrained longing that she quite warmed to him again.

He held to this attitude, devoted, quietly affectionate; till her sense of rebellion passed away and her real pleasure in his improvement reasserted itself. As they read together, if now and then his arm stole around her waist, he always withdrew it when so commanded. Still, one cannot put the same severity into a prohibition too often repeated. The constant, thoughtful attention of a man experienced in the art of pleasing women, the new and frankly inexperienced efforts he made to meet her highest thoughts, to learn and share her preferences, both pleased her.

He was certainly good looking, certainly amusing, certainly had become a better man from her companionship. She grew to feel a sort of ownership in this newly arisen character; a sort of pride in it. Then, she had always been fond of Morton, since the time when he was only "Susie's big brother." That counted.

Another thing counted, too, counted heavily, though Vivian never dreamed of it and would have hotly repudiated the charge. She was a woman of full marriageable age, with all the unused powers of her woman's nature calling for expression, quite unrecognized.

He was a man who loved her, loved her more deeply than he had ever loved before, than he had even known he could love; who quite recognized what called within him and meant to meet the call. And he was near her every day.

After that one fierce outbreak he held himself well in check. He knew he had startled her then, almost lost her. And with every hour of their companionship he felt more and more how much she was to him. Other women he had pursued, overtaken, left behind. He felt that there was something in Vivian which was beyond him, giving a stir and lift of aspiration which he genuinely enjoyed.

Day by day he strove to win her full approval, and day by day he did not neglect the tiny, slow-lapping waves of little tendernesses, small affectionate liberties at well-chosen moments, always promptly withdrawing when forbidden, but always beginning again a little further on.

Dr. Bellair went to Dr. Hale's office and sat herself down solidly in the patient's chair.

"Dick," she said, "are you going to stand for this?"

"Stand for what, my esteemed but cryptic fellow-practitioner?"

She eyed his calm, reserved countenance with friendly admiration. "You are an awfully good fellow, Dick, but dull. At the same time dull and transparent. Are you going to sit still and let that dangerous patient of yours marry the finest girl in town?"

"Your admiration for girls is always stronger than mine, Jane; and I have, if you will pardon the boast, more than one patient."

"All right, Dick—if you want it made perfectly clear to your understanding. Do you mean to let Morton Elder marry Vivian Lane?"

"What business is it of mine?" he demanded, more than brusquely—savagely.

"You know what he's got."

"I am a physician, not a detective. And I am not Miss Lane's father, brother, uncle or guardian."

"Or lover," added Dr. Bellair, eyeing him quietly. She thought she saw a second's flicker of light in the deep gray eyes, a possible tightening of set lips. "Suppose you are not," she said; "nor even a humanitarian. You *are* a member of society. Do you mean to let a man whom you know has no right to marry, poison the life of that splendid girl?"

He was quite silent for a moment, but she could see the hand on the farther arm of his chair grip it till the nails were white.

"How do you know he—wishes to marry her?"

"If you were about like other people, you old hermit, you'd know it as well as anybody. I think they are on the verge of an engagement, if they aren't over it already. Once more, Dick, shall you do anything?"

"No," said he. Then, as she did not add a word, he rose and walked up and down the office in big strides, turning upon her at last.

"You know how I feel about this. It is a matter of honor—professional honor. You women don't seem to know what the word means. I've told that good-for-nothing young wreck that he has no right to marry for years yet, if ever. That is all I can do. I will not betray the confidence of a patient."

"Not if he had smallpox, or scarlet fever, or the bubonic plague? Suppose a patient of yours had the leprosy, and wanted to marry your sister, would you betray his confidence?"

"I might kill my sister," he said, glaring at her. "I refuse to argue with you."

"Yes, I think you'd better refuse," she said, rising. "And you don't have to kill Vivian Lane, either. A man's honor always seems to want to kill a woman to satisfy it. I'm glad I haven't got the feeling. Well, Dick, I thought I'd give you a chance to come to your senses, a real good chance. But I won't leave you to the pangs of unavailing remorse, you poor old goose. That young syphilitic is no patient of mine." And she marched off to perform a difficult duty.

She was very fond of Vivian. The girl's unselfish sweetness of character and the depth of courage and power she perceived behind the sensitive, almost timid exterior, appealed to her. If she had had a daughter, perhaps she would have been like that. If she had had a daughter would she not have thanked anyone who would try to save her from such a danger? From that worse than deadly peril, because of which she had no daughter.

Dr. Bellair was not the only one who watched Morton's growing devotion with keen interest. To his aunt it was a constant joy. From the time her boisterous little nephew had come to rejoice her heart and upset her immaculate household arrangements, and had played, pleasantly though tyrannically, with the little girl next door, Miss Orella had dreamed this romance for him. To have it fail was part of her grief when he left her, to have it now so visibly coming to completion was a deep delight.

If she had been blind to his faults, she was at least vividly conscious of the present sudden growth of virtues. She beamed at him with affectionate pride, and her manner to Mrs. Pettigrew was one of barely subdued "I told you so." Indeed, she could not restrain herself altogether, but spoke to that lady with tender triumph of how lovely it was to have Morton so gentle and nice.

"You never did like the boy, I know, but you must admit that he is behaving beautifully now."

"I will," said the old lady; "I'll admit it without reservation. He's behaving beautifully—now. But I'm not going to talk about him—to you, Orella." So she rolled up her knitting work and marched off.

"Too bad she's so prejudiced and opinionated," said Miss Elder to Susie, rather warmly. "I'm real fond of Mrs. Pettigrew, but when she takes a dislike—"

Susie was so happy herself that she seemed to walk in an aura of rosy light. Her Jimmie was so evidently the incarnation of every masculine virtue and charm that he lent a reflected lustre to other men, even to her brother. Because of her love for Jimmie, she loved Morton better—loved everybody better. To have her only brother marry her dearest friend was wholly pleasant to Susie.

It was not difficult to wring from Vivian a fair knowledge of how things stood, for, though reserved by nature, she was utterly unused to concealing anything, and could not tell an efficient lie if she wanted to.

"Are you engaged or are you not, you dear old thing?" demanded Susie.

And Vivian admitted that there was "an understanding." But Susie absolutely must not speak of it.

For a wonder she did not, except to Jimmie. But people seemed to make up their minds on the subject with miraculous agreement. The general interest in the manifold successes of Mrs. St. Cloud gave way to this vivid personal interest, and it was discussed from two sides among their whole circle of acquaintance.

One side thought that a splendid girl was being wasted, sacrificed, thrown away, on a disagreeable, good-for-nothing fellow. The other side thought the "interesting" Mr. Elder might have done better; they did not know what he could see in her.

They, that vaguely important They, before whom we so deeply bow, were also much occupied in their mind by speculations concerning Mr. Dykeman and two Possibilities. One quite patently possible, even probable, giving rise to the complacent "Why, anybody could see that!" and the other a fascinatingly impossible Possibility of a sort which allows the even more complacent "Didn't you? Why, I could see it from the first."

Mr. Dykeman had been a leading citizen in that new-built town for some ten years, which constituted him almost the Oldest Inhabitant. He was reputed to be extremely wealthy, though he never said anything about it, and neither his clothing nor his cigars reeked of affluence. Perhaps nomadic chambermaids had spread knowledge of those silver-backed appurtenances, and the long mirror. Or perhaps it was not women's gossip at all, but men's gossip, which has wider base, and wider circulation, too.

Mr. Dykeman had certainly "paid attentions" to Miss Elder. Miss Elder had undeniably brightened and blossomed most becomingly under these attentions. He had danced with her, he had driven with her, he had played piquet with her when he might have played whist. To be sure, he did these things with other ladies, and had done them for years past, but this really looked as if there might be something in it.

Mr. Skee, as Mr. Dykeman's oldest friend, was even questioned a little; but it was not very much use to question Mr. Skee. His manner was not repellant, and not in the least reserved. He poured forth floods of information so voluminous and so varied that the recipient was rather drowned than fed. So opinions wavered as to Mr. Dykeman's intentions.

Then came this lady of irresistible charm, and the unmarried citizens of the place fell at her feet as one man. Even the married ones slanted over a little.

Mr. Dykeman danced with her, more than he had with Miss Elder. Mr. Dykeman drove with her, more than he had with Miss Elder. Mr. Dykeman played piquet with her, and chess, which Miss Elder could not play. And Miss Elder's little opening petals of ribbon and lace curled up and withered away; while Mrs. St. Cloud's silken efflorescence, softly waving and jewel-starred, flourished apace.

Dr. Bellair had asked Vivian to take a walk with her; and they sat together, resting, on a high lonely hill, a few miles out of town.

"It's a great pleasure to see this much of you, Dr. Bellair," said the girl, feeling really complimented.

"I'm afraid you won't think so, my dear, when you hear what I have to say: what I *have* to say."

The girl flushed a little. "Are you going to scold me about something? Have I done anything wrong?" Her eyes smiled bravely. "Go on, Doctor. I know it will be for my best good."

"It will indeed, dear child," said the doctor, so earnestly that Vivian felt a chill of apprehension.

"I am going to talk to you 'as man to man' as the story books say; as woman to woman. When I was your age I had been married three years."

Vivian was silent, but stole out a soft sympathetic hand and slipped it into the older woman's. She had heard of this early-made marriage, also early broken; with various dark comments to which she had paid no attention.

Dr. Bellair was Dr. Bellair, and she had a reverential affection for her.

There was a little silence. The Doctor evidently found it hard to begin. "You love children, don't you, Vivian?"

The girl's eyes kindled, and a heavenly smile broke over her face. "Better than anything in the world," she said.

"Ever think about them?" asked her friend, her own face whitening as she spoke. "Think about their lovely little soft helplessness—when you hold them in your arms and have to do *everything* for them. Have to go and turn them over—see that the little ear isn't crumpled—that the covers are all right. Can't you see 'em, upside down on the bath apron, grabbing at things, perfectly happy, but prepared to howl when it comes to dressing? And when they are big enough to love you! Little soft arms that will hardly go round your neck. Little soft cheeks against yours, little soft mouths and little soft kisses,—ever think of them?"

The girl's eyes were like stars. She was looking into the future; her breath came quickly; she sat quite still.

The doctor swallowed hard, and went on. "We mostly don't go much farther than that at first. It's just the babies we want. But you can look farther—can follow up, year by year, the lovely changing growing bodies and minds, the confidence and love between you, the pride you have as health is established, strength and skill developed, and character unfolds and deepens.

"Then when they are grown, and sort of catch up, and you have those splendid young lives about you, intimate strong friends and tender lovers. And you feel as though you had indeed done something for the world."

She stopped, saying no more for a little, watching the girl's awed shining face. Suddenly that face was turned to her, full of exquisite sympathy, the dark eyes swimming with sudden tears; and two soft eager arms held her close.

"Oh, Doctor! To care like that and not—!"

"Yes, my dear;" said the doctor, quietly. "And not have any. Not be able to have any—ever."

Vivian caught her breath with pitying intensity, but her friend went on.

"Never be able to have a child, because I married a man who had gonorrhea. In place of happy love, lonely pain. In place of motherhood, disease. Misery and shame, child. Medicine and surgery, and never any possibility of any child for me."

The girl was pale with horror. "I—I didn't know—" She tried to say something, but the doctor burst out impatiently:

"No! You don't know. I didn't know. Girls aren't taught a word of what's before them till it's too late—not *then,* sometimes! Women lose every joy in life, every hope, every capacity for service or pleasure. They go down to their graves without anyone's telling them the cause of it all."

"That was why you—left him?" asked Vivian presently.

"Yes, I left him. When I found I could not be a mother I determined to be a doctor, and save other women, if I could." She said this with such slow, grave emphasis that Vivian turned a sudden startled face to her, and went white to the lips.

"I may be wrong," the doctor said, "you have not given me your confidence in this matter. But it is better, a thousand times better, that I should make this mistake than for you to make that. You must not marry Morton Elder."

Vivian did not admit nor deny. She still wore that look of horror.

"You think he has—That?"

"I do not know whether he has gonorrhea or not; it takes a long microscopic analysis to be sure; but there is every practical assurance that he's had it, and I know he's had syphilis."

If Vivian could have turned paler she would have, then.

"I've heard of—that," she said, shuddering.

"Yes, the other is newer to our knowledge, far commoner, and really more dangerous. They are two of the most terrible diseases known to us; highly contagious, and in the case of syphilis, hereditary. Nearly three-quarters of the men have one or the other, or both."

But Vivian was not listening. Her face was buried in her hands. She crouched low in agonized weeping.

"Oh, come, come, my dear. Don't take it so hard. There's no harm done you see, it's not too late."

"Oh, it *is* too late! It is!" wailed the girl. "I have promised to marry him."

"I don't care if you were at the altar, child; you *haven't* married him, and you mustn't."

"I have given my word!" said the girl dully. She was thinking of Morton now. Of his handsome face, with it's new expression of respectful tenderness; of all the hopes they had built together; of his life, so dependent upon hers for its higher interests.

She turned to the doctor, her lips quivering. "He *loves* me!" she said. "I—we—he says I am all that holds him up, that helps him to make a newer better life. And he has changed so—I can see it! He says he has loved me, really, since he was seventeen!"

The older sterner face did not relax.

"He told me he had—done wrong. He was honest about it. He said he wasn't—worthy."

"He isn't," said Dr. Bellair.

"But surely I owe some duty to him. He depends on me. And I have promised—"

The doctor grew grimmer. "Marriage is for motherhood," she said. "That is its initial purpose. I suppose you might deliberately forego motherhood, and undertake a sort of missionary relation to a man, but that is not marriage."

"He loves me," said the girl with gentle stubbornness. She saw Morton's eyes, as she had so often seen them lately; full of adoration and manly patience. She felt his hand, as she had felt it so often lately, holding hers, stealing about her waist, sometimes bringing her fingers to his lips for a strong slow kiss which she could not forget for hours.

She raised her head. A new wave of feeling swept over her. She saw a vista of self-sacrificing devotion, foregoing much, forgiving much, but rejoicing in the companionship of a noble life, a soul rebuilt, a love that was passionately grateful. Her eyes met those of her friend fairly. "And I love him!" she said.

"Will you tell that to your crippled children?" asked Dr. Bellair. "Will they understand it if they are idiots? Will they see it if they are blind? Will it satisfy you when they are dead?"

The girl shrank before her.

"You *shall* understand," said the doctor. "This is no case for idealism and exalted emotion. Do you want a son like Theophile?"

"I thought you said—they didn't have any."

"Some don't—that is one result. Another result—of gonorrhea—is to have children born blind. Their eyes may be saved, with care. But it is not a motherly gift for one's babies—blindness. You may have years and years of suffering yourself—any or all of those diseases 'peculiar to women' as we used to call them! And we pitied the men who 'were so good to their invalid wives'! You may have any number of still-born children, year after year. And every little marred dead face would remind you that you allowed it! And they may be deformed and twisted, have all manner of terrible and loathsome afflictions, they and their children after them, if they have any. And many do! Dear girl, don't you see that's wicked?"

Vivian was silent, her two hands wrung together; her whole form shivering with emotion.

"Don't think that you are 'ruining his life,' " said the doctor kindly. "He ruined it long ago—poor boy!"

The girl turned quickly at the note of sympathy.

"They don't know either," her friend went on. "What could Miss Orella do, poor little saint, to protect a lively young fellow like that! All they have in their scatter-brained heads is 'it's naughty but it's nice!' And so they rush off and ruin their whole lives—and their wives'—and their children's. A man don't have to be so very wicked, either, understand. Just one mis-step may be enough for infection."

"Even if it did break his heart, and yours—even if you both lived single, he because it is the only decent thing he can do now, you because of a misguided sense of devotion; that would be better than to commit this plain sin. Beware of a biological sin, my dear; for it there is no forgiveness."

She waited a moment and went on, as firmly and steadily as she would have held the walls of a wound while she placed the stitches.

"If you two love each other so nobly and devotedly that it is higher and truer and more lasting than the ordinary love of men and women, you might be 'true' to one another for a lifetime, you see. And all that friendship can do, exalted influence, noble inspiration—that is open to you."

Vivian's eyes were wide and shining. She saw a possible future, not wholly unbearable.

"Has he kissed you yet?" asked the doctor suddenly.

"No," she said. "That is—except—"

"Don't let him. You might catch it. Your friendship must be distant. Well, shall we be going back? I'm sorry, my dear. I did hate awfully to do it. But I hated worse to see you go down those awful steps from which there is no returning."

"Yes," said Vivian. "Thank you. Won't you go on, please? I'll come later."

An hour the girl sat there, with the clear blue sky above her, the soft steady wind rustling the leaves, the little birds that hopped and pecked and flirted their tails so near her motionless figure.

She thought and thought, and through all the tumult of ideas it grew clearer to her that the doctor was right. She might sacrifice herself. She had no right to sacrifice her children.

A feeling of unreasoning horror at this sudden outlook into a field of unknown evil was met by her clear perception that if she was old enough to marry, to be a mother, she was surely old enough to know these things; and not only so, but ought to know them.

Shy, sensitive, delicate in feeling as the girl was, she had a fair and reasoning mind.

10

DETERMINATION

You may shut your eyes with a bandage,
The while world vanishes soon;
You may open your eyes at a knothole
And see the sun and moon.

It must have grieved anyone who cared for Andrew Dykeman, to see Mrs. St. Cloud's manner toward him change with his changed circumstances—she had been so much with him, had been so kind to him; kinder than Carston comment "knew for a fact," but not kinder than it surmised.

Then, though his dress remained as quietly correct, his face assumed a worn and anxious look, and he no longer offered her long auto rides or other expensive entertainment. She saw men on the piazza stop talking as he came by, and shake their heads as they looked after him; but no one would tell her anything definite till she questioned Mr. Skee.

"I am worried about Mr. Dykeman," she said to this ever-willing confidant, beckoning him to a chair beside her.

A chair, to the mind of Mr. Skee, seemed to be for pictorial uses, only valuable as part of the composition. He liked one to stand beside, to put a foot on, to lean over from behind, arms on the back; to tip up in front of him as if he needed a barricade; and when he was persuaded to sit in one, it was either facing the back, cross-saddle and bent forward, or—and this was the utmost decorum he was able to approach—tipped backward against the wall.

"He does not look well," said the lady, "you are old friends—do tell me; if it is anything wherein a woman's sympathy would be of service?"

"I'm afraid not, Ma'am," replied Mr. Skee darkly. "Andy's hard hit in a worse place than his heart. I wouldn't betray a friend's confidence for any money, Ma'am; but this is all over town. It'll go hard with Andy, I'm afraid, at his age."

"Oh, I'm so sorry!" she whispered. "So sorry! But surely with a man of his abilities it will be only a temporary reverse!—"

"Dunno 'bout the abilities—not in this case. Unless he has ability enough to discover a mine bigger'n the one he's lost! You see, Ma'am, it's this way," and he sunk his voice to a confidential rumble. "Andy had a bang-up mine, galena ore—not gold, you understand, but often pays better. And he kept on putting the money it made back into it to make more. Then, all of a sudden, it petered out! No more eggs in that basket. 'Course he can't sell it—now. And last year he refused half a million. Andy's sure down on his luck."

"But he will recover! You western men are so wonderful! He will find another mine!"

"O yes, he *may!* Certainly he *may* Ma'am. Not that he found this one—he just bought it."

"Well—he can buy another, there are more, aren't there?"

"Sure there are! There's as good mines in the earth as ever was salted—that's my motto! But Andy's got no more money to buy any mines. What he had before he inherited. No, Ma'am," said Mr. Skee, with a sigh. "I'm afraid its all up with Andy Dykeman financially!"

This he said more audibly; and Miss Elder and Mrs. Pettigrew, sitting in their parlor, could not help hearing. Miss Elder gave a little gasp and clasped her hands tightly, but Mrs. Pettigrew arose, and came outside.

"What's this about Mr. Dykeman?" she questioned abruptly. "Has he had losses?"

"There now," said Mr. Skee, remorsefully, "I never meant to give him away like that. Mrs. Pettigrew, Ma'am, I must beg you not to mention it further. I was only satisfyin' this lady here, in answer to sympathetic anxiety, as to what was making Andrew H. Dykeman so down in the mouth. Yes'm—he's lost every cent he had in the world, or is likely to have. Of course, among friends, he'll get a job fast enough, bookkeepin', or something like that—though he's not a brilliant man, Andy isn't. You needn't to feel worried, Mrs. Pettigrew; he'll draw a salary all right, to the end of time; but he's out of the game of Hot Finance."

Mrs. Pettigrew regarded the speaker with a scintillating eye. He returned her look with unflinching seriousness. "Have a chair, Ma'am," he said. "Let me bring out your rocker. Sit down and chat with us."

"No, thanks," said the old lady. "It seems to me a little—chilly, out here. I'll go in."

She went in forthwith, to find Miss Orella furtively wiping her eyes.

"What are you crying about, Orella Elder! Just because a man's lost his money? That happens to most of 'em now and then."

"Yes, I know—but you heard what he said. Oh, I can't believe it! To think of his having to be provided for by his friends—and having to take a small salary—after being so well off! I am so sorry for him!"

Miss Elder's sorrow was increased to intensity by noting Mrs. St. Cloud's changed attitude. Mr. Dykeman made no complaint, uttered no protest, gave no confidences; but it soon appeared that he was working in an office; and furthermore that this position was given him by Mr. Skee.

That gentleman, though discreetly reticent as to his own affairs, now appeared in far finer raiment than he had hitherto affected; developed a pronounced taste in fobs and sleeve buttons; and a striking harmony in socks and scarfs.

Men talked openly of him; no one seemed to know anything definite, but all were certain that "Old Skee must have struck it rich."

Mr. Skee kept his own counsel; but became munificent in gifts and entertainments. He produced two imposing presents for Susie; one a "betrothal gift," the other a conventional wedding present.

"This is a new one to me," he said when he offered her the first; "but I understand it's the thing. In fact I'm sure of it—for I've consulted Mrs. St. Cloud and she helped me to buy 'em."

He consulted Mrs. St. Cloud about a dinner he proposed giving to Mr. Saunders—"one of these Farewell to Egypt affairs," he said. "Not that I imagine Jim Saunders ever was much of a—Egyptian—but then—!"

He consulted her also about Vivian—did she not think the girl looked worn and ill? Wouldn't it be a good thing to send her off for a trip somewhere?

He consulted her about a library; said he had always wanted a library of his own, but the public ones were somewhat in his way. How many books did she think a man ought really to own—to spend his declining years among. Also, and at considerable length he consulted her about the best possible place of residence.

"I'm getting to be an old man, Mrs. St. Cloud," he remarked meditatively; "and I'm thinking of buying and building somewhere. But it's a ticklish job. Lo! these many years I've been perfectly contented to live wherever I was at; and now that I'm considering a real Home—blamed if I know where to put it! I'm distracted between A Model Farm, and A Metropolitan Residence. Which would you recommend, Ma'am?"

The lady's sympathy and interest warmed to Mr. Skee as they cooled to Mr. Dykeman, not with any blameworthy or noticeable suddenness, but in soft graduations, steady and continuous. The one wore his new glories with an air of modest pride; making no boast of affluence; and the other accepted that which had befallen him without rebellion.

Miss Orella's tender heart was deeply touched. As fast as Mrs. St. Cloud gave the cold shoulder to her friend, she extended a warm hand; when they chatted about Mr. Skee's visible success, she spoke bravely of the beauty of limited means; and when it was time to present her weekly bills to the boarders, she left none in Mr. Dykeman's room. This he took for an oversight at first; but when he found the omission repeated on the following week, he stood by his window smiling thoughtfully for some time, and then went in search of Miss Orella.

She sat by her shaded lamp, alone, knitting a silk tie which was promptly hidden as he entered. He stood by the door looking at her in spite of her urging him to be seated, observing the warm color in her face, the graceful lines of her figure, the gentle smile that was so unfailingly attractive. Then he came forward, calmly inquiring, "Why haven't you sent me my board bill?"

She lifted her eyes to his, and dropped them, flushing. "I—excuse me; but I thought—"

"You thought I couldn't conveniently pay it?"

"O please excuse me! I didn't mean to be—to do anything you wouldn't like. But I did hear that your were—temporarily embarrassed. And I want you to feel sure, Mr. Dykeman, that to your real friends it makes no difference in the *least.* And if—for a while that is—it should be a little more convenient to—to defer payment, please feel perfectly at liberty to wait!"

She stood there blushing like a girl, her sweet eyes wet with shining tears that did not fall, full of tender sympathy for his misfortune.

"Have you heard that I've lost all my money?" he asked.

She nodded softly.

"And that I can't ever get it back—shall have to do clerk's work at a clerk's salary—as long as I live?"

Again she nodded.

He took a step or two back and forth in the quiet parlor, and returned to her.

"Would you marry a poor man?" he asked in a low tender voice. "Would you marry a man not young, not clever, not rich, but who loved you dearly? You are the sweetest woman I ever saw, Orella Elder—will you marry me?"

She came to him, and he drew her close with a long sigh of utter satisfaction. "Now I am rich indeed," he said softly.

She held him off a little. "Don't talk about being rich. It doesn't matter. If you like to live here—why this house will keep us both. If you'd rather have a little one—I can live *so* happily—on *so* little! And there is my own little home in Bainville—perhaps you could find something to do there. I don't care the least in the world—so long as you love me!"

"I've loved you since I first set eyes on you," he answered her. "To see the home you've made here for all of us was enough to make any man love you. But I thought awhile back that I hadn't any chance—you weren't jealous of that Artificial Fairy, were you?"

And conscientiously Miss Orella lied.

Carston society was pleased, but not surprised at Susie's engagement; it was both pleased and surprised when Miss Elder's was announced. Some there were who protested that they had seen it from the beginning; but disputatious friends taxed them with having prophesied quite otherwise.

Some thought Miss Elder foolish to take up with a man of full middle age, and with no prospects; and others attributed the foolishness to Mr. Dykeman, in marrying an old maid. Others again darkly hinted that he knew which side his bread was buttered—"and first-rate butter, too." Adding that they "did hate to see a man sit around and let his wife keep boarders!"

In Bainville circles the event created high commotion. That one of their accumulated maidens, part of the Virgin Sacrifice of New England, which finds not even a Minotaur—had thus triumphantly escaped from their ranks and achieved a husband; this was flatly heretical. The fact that he was a poor man was the only mitigating circumstance, leaving it open to the more captious to criticize the lady sharply.

But the calm contentment of Andrew Dykeman's face, and the decorous bliss of Miss Elder's were untroubled by what anyone thought or said.

Little Susie was delighted, and teased for a double wedding; without success. "One was enough to attend to, at one time," her aunt replied.

IN ALL THIS atmosphere of wooings and weddings, Vivian walked apart, as one in a bad dream that could never end. That day when Dr. Bellair left her on the hill, left her alone in a strange new horrible world, was still glaring across her consciousness, the end of one life, the bar to any other. Its small events were as clear to her as those which stand out so painfully on a day of death; all that led up to the pleasant walk, when an eager girl mounted the breezy height, and a sad-faced woman came down from it.

She had waited long and came home slowly, dreading to see a face she knew, dreading worst of all to see Morton. The boy she had known so long, the man she was beginning to know, had changed to an unbelievable horror; and the love which had so lately seemed real to her recoiled upon her heart with a sense of hopeless shame.

She wished—eagerly, desperately, she wished—she need never see him again. She thought of the man's resource of running away—if she could just *go,* go at once, and write to him from somewhere.

Distant Bainville seemed like a haven of safety; even the decorous, narrow, monotony of its dim life had a new attraction. These terrors were not in Bainville, surely. Then the sickening thought crept in that perhaps they were—only they did not know it. Besides, she had no money to go with. If only she had started that little school sooner! Write to her father for money she would not. No, she must bear it here.

The world was discolored in the girl's eyes. Love had become a horror and marriage impossible. She pushed the idea from her, impotently, as one might push at a lava flow.

In her wide reading she had learned in a vague way of "evil"—a distant undescribed evil which was in the world, and which must be avoided. She had known that there was such a thing as "sin," and abhorred the very thought of it.

Morton's penitential confessions had given no details; she had pictured him only as being "led astray," as being "fast," even perhaps "wicked." Wickedness could be forgiven; and she had forgiven him, royally. But wickedness was one thing, disease was another. Forgiveness was no cure.

The burden of new knowledge so distressed her that she avoided the family entirely that evening, avoided Susie, went to her grandmother and asked if she might come and sleep on the lounge in her room.

"Surely, my child, glad to have you," said Mrs. Pettigrew affectionately. "Better try my bed—there's room a-plenty."

The girl lay long with those old arms about her, crying quietly. Her grandmother asked no questions, only patted her softly from time to time, and said, "There! There!" in a pleasantly soothing manner. After some time she remarked, "If you want to say things, my dear, say 'em—anything you please."

In the still darkness they talked long and intimately; and the wise old head straightened things out somewhat for the younger one.

"Doctors don't realize how people feel about these matters," said Mrs. Pettigrew. "They are so used to all kinds of ghastly things they forget that other folks can't stand 'em. She was too hard on you, dearie."

But Vivian defended the doctor. "Oh, no, Grandma. She did it beautifully. And it hurt her so. She told me about her own—disappointment."

"Yes, I remember her as a girl, you see. A fine sweet girl she was too. It was an awful blow—and she took it hard. It has made her bitter, I think, perhaps; that and the number of similar cases she had to cope with."

"But, Grandma—is it—*can* it be as bad as she said? Seventy-five per cent! Three-quarters of—of everybody!"

"Not everybody, dear; thank goodness. Our girls are mostly clean, and they save the race, I guess."

"I don't even want to *see* a man again!" said the girl with low intensity.

"Shouldn't think you would, at first. But, dear child—just brace yourself and look it fair in the face! The world's no worse than it was yesterday—just because you know more about it!"

"No," Vivian admitted, "But it's like uncovering a charnel house!" she shuddered.

"Never saw a charnel house myself," said the old lady, "even with the lid on. But now see here, child; you mustn't feel as if all men were Unspeakable Villains. They are just ignorant boys—and nobody ever tells 'em the truth. Nobody used to know it, for that matter. All this about gonorrhea is quite newly discovered—it has set the doctors all by the ears. Having women doctors has made a difference too—lots of difference."

"Besides," she went on after a pause, "things are changing very fast now, since the general airing began. Dr. Prince Morrow in New York, with that society of his—(I can never remember the name—makes me think of tooth-brushes) has done much; and the popular magazines have taken it up. You must have seen some of those articles, Vivian."

"I have," the girl said, "but I couldn't bear to read them—ever."

"That's it!" responded her grandmother, tartly; "we bring up girls to think it is not proper to know anything about the worst danger before them. Proper!—Why my dear child, the young girls are precisely the ones *to* know! It's no use to tell a woman who has buried all her children—or wishes she had!—that it was all owing to her ignorance, and her husband's. You have to know beforehand if it's to do you any good."

After awhile she continued: "Women are waking up to this all over the country, now. Nice women, old and young. The women's clubs and congresses are taking it up, as they should. Some states have passed laws requiring a medical certificate—a clean bill of health—to go with a license to marry. You can see that's reasonable! A man has to be examined to enter the army or navy, even to get his life insured; Marriage and Parentage are more important than those things! And we are beginning to teach children and young people what they ought to know. There's hope for us!"

"But Grandma—it's so awful—about the children."

"Yes, dear, yes. It's pretty awful. But don't feel as if we were all on the brink of perdition. Remember that we've got a whole quarter of the men to bank on. That's a good many, in this country. We're not so bad as Europe—not yet—in this line. Then just think of this, child. We have lived, and done splendid things all these years, even with this load of disease on us. Think what we can do when we're rid of it! And that's in the hands of women, my dear—as soon as we know enough. Don't be afraid of knowledge. When we all know about this we can stop it! Think of that. We can religiously rid the world of all these—'undesirable citizens.'"

"How, Grandma?"

"Easy enough, my dear. By not marrying them."

There was a lasting silence.

Grandma finally went to sleep, making a little soft whistling sound through her parted lips; but Vivian lay awake for long slow hours.

IT WAS ONE thing to make up her own mind, though not an easy one, by any means; it was quite another to tell Morton.

He gave her no good opportunity. He did not say again, "Will you marry me?" So that she could say, "No," and be done with it. He did not even say, "When will you marry me?" to which she could answer "Never!" He merely took it for granted that she was going to, and continued to monopolize her as far as possible, with all pleasant and comfortable attentions.

She forced the situation even more sharply than she wished, by turning from him with a shiver when he met her on the stairs one night and leaned forward as if to kiss her.

He stopped short.

"What is the matter, Vivian—are you ill?"

"No—" She could say nothing further, but tried to pass him.

"Look here—there *is* something. You've been—different—for several days. Have I done anything you don't like?"

"Oh, Morton!" His question was so exactly to the point; and so exquisitely inadequate! He had indeed.

"I care too much for you to let anything stand between us, now," he went on.

"Come, there's no one in the upper hall—come and 'tell me the worst.' "

"As well now as ever," thought the girl. Yet when they sat on the long window seat, and he turned his handsome face toward her, with that newer, better look on it, she could not believe that this awful thing was true.

"Now then—What is wrong between us?" he said.

She answered only, "I will tell you the worst, Morton. I cannot marry you—ever."

He whitened to the lips, but asked quietly, "Why?"

"Because you have—Oh, I *cannot* tell you!"

"I have a right to know, Vivian. You have made a man of me. I love you with my whole heart. What have I done—that I have not told you?"

Then she recalled his contrite confessions; and contrasted what he had told her with what he had not; with the unspeakable fate to which he would have consigned her—and those to come; and a sort of holy rage rose within her.

"You never told me of the state of your health, Morton."

It was done. She looked to see him fall at her feet in utter abashment, but he did nothing of the kind. What he did do astonished her beyond measure. He rose to his feet, with clenched fists.

"Has that damned doctor been giving me away?" he demanded. "Because if he has I'll kill him!"

"He has not," said Vivian. "Not by the faintest hint, ever. And is *that* all you think of?—

"Good-bye."

She rose to leave him, sick at heart.

Then he seemed to realize that she was going; that she meant it.

"Surely, surely!" he cried, "you won't throw me over now! Oh, Vivian! I told you I had been wild—that I wasn't fit to touch your little slippers! And I wasn't going to ask you to marry me till I felt sure this was all done with. All the rest of my life was yours, darling—is yours. You have made me over—surely you won't leave me now!"

"I must," she said.

He looked at her despairingly. If he lost her he lost not only a woman, but the hope of a life. Things he had never thought about before had now grown dear to him; a home, a family, an honorable place in the world, long years of quiet happiness.

"I can't lose you!" he said. "I *can't!*"

She did not answer, only sat there with a white set face and her hands tight clenched in her lap.

"Where'd you get this idea anyhow?" he burst out again. "I believe it's that woman doctor! What does she know!"

"Look here, Morton," said Vivian firmly. "It is not a question of who told me. The important thing is that it's—true! And I cannot marry you."

"But Vivian—" he pleaded, trying to restrain the intensity of his feeling; "men get over these things. They do, really. It's not so awful as you seem to think. It's very common. And I'm nearly well. I was going to wait a year or two yet—to make sure—. Vivian! I'd cut my hand off before I'd hurt you!"

There was real agony in his voice, and her heart smote her; but there was something besides her heart ruling the girl now.

"I am sorry—I'm very sorry," she said dully. "But I will not marry you."

"You'll throw me over—just for that! Oh, Vivian don't—you can't. I'm no worse than other men. It seems so terrible to you just because you're so pure and white. It's only what they call—wild oats, you know. Most men do it."

She shook her head.

"And will you punish me—so cruelly—for that? I can't live without you, Vivian—I won't!"

"It is not a question of punishing you, Morton," she said gently. "Nor myself. It is not the sin I am considering. It is the consequences!"

He felt something high and implacable in the gentle girl; something he had never found in her before. He looked at her with despairing eyes. Her white grace, her stately little ways, her delicate beauty, had never seemed so desirable.

"Good God, Vivian. You can't mean it. Give me time. Wait for me.

I'll be straight all the rest of my life—I mean it. I'll be true to you, absolutely. I'll do anything you say—only don't give me up!"

She felt old, hundreds of years old, and as remote as far mountains.

"It isn't anything you can do—in the rest of your life, my poor boy! It is what you have done—in the first of it! . . . Oh, Morton! It isn't right to let us grow up without knowing! You never would have done it *if* you'd known—would you? Can't you—can't we—do something to—stop this awfulness?"

Her tender heart suffered in the pain she was inflicting, suffered too in her own loss; for as she faced the thought of final separation she found that her grief ran back into the far-off years of childhood. But she had made up her mind with a finality only the more absolute because it hurt her. Even what he said of possible recovery did not move her—the very thought of marriage had become impossible.

"I shall never marry," she added, with a shiver; thinking that he might derive some comfort from the thought; but he replied with a bitter derisive little laugh. He did not rise to her appeal to "help the others." So far in life the happiness of Morton Elder had been his one engrossing care; and now the unhappiness of Morton Elder assumed even larger proportions.

That bright and hallowed future to which he had been looking forward so earnestly had been suddenly withdrawn from him; his good resolutions, his "living straight" for the present, were wasted.

"You women that are so superior," he said, "that'll turn a man down for things that are over and done with—that he's sorry for and ashamed of—do you know what you drive a man to! What do you think's going to become of me if you throw me over!"

He reached out his hands to her in real agony. "Vivian! I love you! I can't live without you! I can't be good without you! And you love me a little—don't you?"

She did. She could not deny it. She loved to shut her eyes to the future, to forgive the past, to come to those outstretched arms and bury everything beneath that one overwhelming phrase—"I love you!"

But she heard again Dr. Bellair's clear low accusing voice—"Will you tell that to your crippled children?"

She rose to her feet. "I cannot help it, Morton. I am sorry—you will not believe how sorry I am! But I will never marry you."

A look of swift despair swept over his face. It seemed to darken visibly as she watched. An expression of bitter hatred came upon him; of utter recklessness.

All that the last few months had seemed to bring of higher better feeling fell from him; and even as she pitied him she thought with a flicker of fear of how this might have happened—after marriage.

"Oh, well!" he said, rising to his feet. "I wish you could have made up your mind sooner, that's all. I'll take myself off now."

She reached out her hands to him.

"Morton! Please!—don't go away feeling so hardly! I am—fond of you—I always was.—Won't you let me help you—to bear it—! Can't we be—friends?"

Again he laughed that bitter little laugh. "No, Miss Lane," he said. "We distinctly cannot. This is good-bye—You won't change your mind—again?"

She shook her head in silence, and he left her.

11

THEREAFTER

If I do right, though heavens fall,
  And end all light and laughter;
Though black the night and ages long,
  Bitter the cold—the tempest strong—
If I do right, and brave it all—
  The sun shall rise thereafter!

The inaccessibility of Dr. Hale gave him, in the eye of Mrs. St. Cloud, all the attractiveness of an unscaled peak to the true mountain climber. Here was a man, an unattached man, living next door to her, whom she had not even seen. Her pursuance of what Mr. Skee announced to his friends to be "one of these Platonic Friendships," did not falter; neither did her interest in other relations less philosophic. Mr. Dykeman's precipitate descent from the class of eligibles was more of a disappointment to her than she would admit even to herself; his firm, kind friendliness had given a sense of comfort, of achieved content that her restless spirit missed.

But Dr. Hale, if he had been before inaccessible, had now become so heavily fortified, so empanoplied in armor offensive and defensive, that even Mrs. Pettigrew found it difficult to obtain speech with him.

That his best friend, so long supporting him in cheerful bachelorhood, should have thus late laid down his arms, was bitterly resented. That Mr. Skee, free lance of years standing, and risen victor from several "stricken fields," should show signs of capitulation, annoyed him further. Whether these feelings derived their intensity from another, which he entirely refused to acknowledge, is matter for the psychologist, and Dr. Hale avoided all psychologic self-examination.

With the boys he was always a hero. They admired his quiet strength and the unbroken good nature that was always presented to those about him, whatever his inner feelings.

Mr. Peters burst forth to the others one day, in tones of impassioned admiration.

"By George, fellows," he said, "you know how nice Doc was last night?"

"Never saw him when he wasn't," said Archie.

"Don't interrupt Mr. Peters," drawled Percy. "He's on the brink of a scientific discovery. Strange how these secrets of nature can lie unrevealed about us so long—and then suddenly burst upon our ken!"

Mr. Peters grinned affably. "That's all right, but I maintain my assertion; whatever the general attraction of our noble host, you'll admit that on the special occasion of yesterday evening, which we celebrated to a late hour by innocent games of cards—he was—as usual—the soul of—of—"

"Affability?" suggested Percy.

"Precisely!" Peters admitted. "If there is a well-chosen word which perfectly describes the manner of Dr. Richard Hale—it is affable! Thank you, sir, thank you. Well, what I wish to announce, so that you can all of you get down on your knees at once and worship, is that all last evening he—had a toothache—a bad toothache!"

"My word!" said Archie, and remained silent.

"Oh, come now," Percy protested, "that's against nature. Have a toothache and not *mention* it? Not even mention it—without exaggeration! Why Archimedes couldn't do that! Or—Sandalphon—or any of them!"

"How'd you learn the facts, my son? Tell us that."

"Heard him on the 'phone making an appointment. 'Yes;' 'since noon yesterday,' 'yes, pretty severe.' '11:30? You can't make it earlier? All right.' I'm just mentioning it to convince you fellows that you don't appreciate your opportunities. There was some exceptional Female once—they said 'to know her was a liberal education.' What would you call it to live with Dr. Hale?"

And they called it every fine thing they could think of; for these boys knew better than anyone else, the effect of that association.

His patients knew him as wise, gentle, efficient, bringing a sense of hope and assurance by the mere touch of that strong hand; his professional associates in the town knew him as a good practitioner and friend, and wider medical circles, readers of his articles in the professional press had an even higher opinion of his powers.

Yet none of these knew Richard Hale. None saw him sitting late in his office, the pages of his book unturned, his eyes on the red spaces of the fire. No one was with him on those night tramps that left but an hour or two of sleep to the long night, and made that sleep irresistible from self-enforced fatigue. He had left the associations of his youth and deliberately selected this far-off mountain town to build the life he chose; and if he found it unsatisfying no one was the wiser.

His successive relays of boys, young fellows fresh from the East, coming from year to year and going from year to year as business called them, could and did give good testimony as to the home side of his character, however. It was not in nature that they should speculate about him. As they fell in love and out again with the facility of so many Romeos, they discoursed among themselves as to his misogyny.

"He certainly has a grouch on women," they would admit. "That's the one thing you can't talk to him about—shuts up like a clam. Of course, he'll let you talk about your own feelings and experiences, but you might as well talk to the side of a hill. I wonder what did happen to him?"

They made no inquiry, however. It was reported that a minister's wife, a person of determined character, had had the courage of her inquisitiveness, and asked him once, "Why is it that you have never married, Dr. Hale?" And that he had replied, "It is owing to my dislike of the meddlesomeness of women." He lived his own life, unquestioned, now more markedly withdrawn than ever, coming no more to The Cottonwood.

Even when Morton Elder left, suddenly and without warning, to the great grief of his aunt and astonishment of his sister, their medical neighbor still "sulked in his tent"—or at least in his office.

Morton's departure had but one explanation; it must be that Vivian had refused him, and she did not deny it.

"But why, Vivian, why? He has improved so—it was just lovely to see how nice he was getting. And we all thought you were so happy." Thus the perplexed Susie. And Vivian found herself utterly unable to explain to that happy little heart, on the brink of marriage, why she had refused her brother.

Miss Orella was even harder to satisfy. "It's not as if you were a foolish changeable young girl, my dear. And you've known Morton all your life—he was no stranger to you. It breaks my heart, Vivian. Can't you reconsider?"

The girl shook her head.

"I'm awfully sorry, Miss Orella. Please believe that I did it for the best—and that it was very hard for me, too."

"But, Vivian! What can be the reason? I don't think you understand what a beautiful influence you have on the boy. He has improved so, since he has been here. And he was going to get a position here in town—he told me so himself—and really settle down. And now he's *gone.* Just off and away, as he used to be—and I never shall feel easy about him again."

Miss Orella was frankly crying; and it wrung the girl's heart to know the pain she was causing; not only to Morton, and to herself, but to these others.

Susie criticised her with frankness.

"I know you think you are right, Vivian, you always do—you and that conscience of yours. But I really think you had gone too far to draw back. Jimmie saw him that night he went away—and he said he looked awfully. And he really was changed so—beginning to be so thoroughly nice. Whatever was the matter? I think you ought to tell me, Vivian, I'm his sister, and—being engaged and all—perhaps I could straighten it out."

And she was as nearly angry as her sunny nature allowed, when her friend refused to give any reason, beyond that she thought it right.

Her aunt did not criticise, but pleaded. "It's not too late, I'm sure, Vivian. A word from you would bring him back in a moment. Do speak it, Vivian—do! Put your pride in your pocket, child, and don't lose a lifetime's happiness for some foolish quarrel."

Miss Orella, like Susie, was at present sure that marriage must mean a lifetime's happiness. And Vivian looked miserably from one to the other of these loving womenfolk, and could not defend herself with the truth.

Mrs. Pettigrew took up the cudgels for her. She was not going to have her favorite grandchild thus condemned and keep silence. "Anybody'd think Vivian had married the man and then run away with another one!" she said tartly. "Pity if a girl can't change her mind before marrying—she's held down pretty close afterward. An engagement isn't a wedding, Orella Elder."

"But you don't consider the poor boy's feelings in the least, Mrs. Pettigrew."

"No, I don't," snapped the old lady. "I consider the poor girl's. I'm willing to bet as much as you will that his feelings aren't any worse than hers. If *he'd* changed his mind and run off and left *her,* I warrant you two wouldn't have been so hard on him."

Evading this issue, Miss Orella wiped her eyes, and said: "Heaven knows where he is now. And I'm afraid he won't write—he never did write much, and now he's just heartbroken. I don't know as I'd have seen him at all if I hadn't been awake and heard him rushing downstairs. You've no idea how he suffers."

"I don't see as the girl's to blame that he hadn't decency enough to say good-bye to the aunt that's been a mother to him; or to write to her, as he ought to. A person don't need to forget *all* their duty because they've got the mitten."

Vivian shrank away from them all. Her heart ached intolerably. She had not realized how large a part in her life this constant admiration and attention had become. She missed the outward agreeableness, and the soft tide of affection, which had risen more and more warmly about her. From her earliest memories she had wished for affection—affection deep and continuous, tender and with full expression. She had been too reserved to show her feeling, too proud by far to express it, but under that delicate reticence of hers lay always that deep longing to love and to be loved wholly.

Susie had been a comfort always, in her kittenish affection and caressing ways, but Susie was doubly lost, both in her new absorption and now in this estrangement.

Then, to bring pain to Miss Orella, who had been so kind and sweet to her from earliest childhood, to hurt her so deeply, now, to mingle in her cup of happiness this grief and anxiety, made the girl suffer keenly. Jimmie, of course, was able to comfort Susie. He told her it was no killing matter anyhow, and that Morton would inevitably console himself elsewhere. "He'll never wear the willow for any girl, my dear. Don't you worry about him."

Also, Mr. Dykeman comforted Miss Orella, not only with wise words, but with his tender sympathy and hopefulness. But no one could comfort Vivian.

Even Dr. Bellair seemed to her present sensitiveness an alien, cruel power. She had come like the angel with the flaming sword to stand between her and what, now that it was gone, began to look like Paradise.

She quite forgot that she had always shrunk from Morton when he made love too warmly, that she had been far from wholly pleased with him when he made his appearance there, that their engagement, so far as they had one, was tentative—"sometime, when I am good enough" not having arrived. The unreasoning voice of the woman's nature within her had answered, though but partially, to the deep call of the man's; and now she missed more than she would admit to herself the tenderness that was gone.

She had her intervals of sharp withdrawal from the memory of that tenderness, of deep thanksgiving for her escape; but fear of a danger only prophesied, does not obliterate memory of joys experienced.

Her grandmother watched her carefully, saying little. She forced no confidence, made no comment, was not obtrusively affectionate, but formed a definite decision and conveyed it clearly to Dr. Bellair.

"Look here, Jane Bellair, you've upset Vivian's dish, and quite right; it's a good thing you did, and I don't know as you could have done it easier."

"I couldn't have done it harder—that I know of," the doctor answered. "I'd sooner operate on a baby—without an anæsthetic—than tell a thing like that—to a girl like that. But it had to be done; and nobody else would."

"You did perfectly right. I'm thankful enough, I promise you; if you hadn't I should have had to—and goodness knows what a mess I'd have made. But look here, the girl's going all to pieces. Now we've got to do something for her, and do it quick."

"I know that well enough," answered her friend, "and I set about it even before I made the incision. You've seen that little building going up on the corner of High and Stone Streets?"

"That pretty little thing with the grass and flowers round it?"

"Yes—they got the flowers growing while the decorators finished inside. It's a first-rate little kindergarten. I've got a list of scholars all arranged for, and am going to pop the girl into it so fast she can't refuse. Not that I think she will."

"Who did it?" demanded Mrs. Pettigrew. "That man Skee?"

"Mr. Skee has had something to do with it," replied the doctor, guardedly; "but he doesn't want his name mentioned."

"Huh!" said Mrs. Pettigrew.

Vivian made no objection, though she was too listless to take up work with enthusiasm.

As a prescription nothing could have worked better. Enough small pupils were collected to pay the rent of the pretty place, and leave a modest income for her.

Dr. Bellair gathered together the mothers and aunts for a series of afternoon talks in the convenient building, Vivian assisting, and roused much interest among them. The loving touch of little hands, the pleasure of seeing the gay contentment of her well-ordered charges, began to lighten the girl's heart at last. They grew so fond of her that the mothers were jealous, but she played with and taught them so wisely, and the youngsters were so much improved by it, that no parent withdrew her darling.

Further than that, the new interest, the necessary reading and study, above all the steady hours of occupation acted most beneficently, slowly, but surely steadying the nerves and comforting the heart.

There is a telling Oriental phrase describing sorrow: "And the whole world became strait unto him." The sense of final closing down of life, of a dull, long, narrow path between her and the grave, which had so oppressed the girl's spirit, now changed rapidly. Here was room to love at least, and she radiated a happy and unselfish affection among the little ones. Here was love in return, very sweet and honest, if shallow. Here was work; something to do, something to think about; both in her hours with the children and those spent in study. Her work took her out of the house, too; away from Susie and her aunt, with their happy chatter and endless white needlework, and the gleeful examination of presents.

Never before had she known the blessed relief of another place to go to.

When she left The Cottonwoods, as early as possible, and placed her key in the door of the little gray house sitting among the roses, she felt a distinct lightening of the heart. This was hers. Not her father's, not Miss Elder's; not anybody's but hers—as long as she could earn the rent.

She paid her board, too, in spite of deep and pained remonstrance, forcing Miss Elder to accept it by the ultimatum "would you rather make me go away and board somewhere else?" She could not accept favors where she was condemned.

This, too, gave her a feeling hitherto inexperienced, deep and inspiring. She began to hold her graceful head insensibly higher, to walk with a freer step. Life was not ended after all, though Love had gone. She might not be happy, but she might be useful and independent.

Then Dr. Bellair, who had by quiet friendliness and wise waiting, regained much of her former place with the girl, asked her to undertake, as a special favor to her, the care of a class of rather delicate children and young girls, in physical culture.

"Of course, Johanna Johnson is perfectly reliable and an excellent teacher. I don't know a better; but their mothers will feel easier if there's someone they know on the spot. You keep order and see that they don't overdo. You'll have to go through their little exercises with them, you see. I can't pay you anything for it; but it's only part of two afternoons in the week—and it won't hurt you at any rate."

Vivian was more than glad to do something for the doctor, as well as to extend her friendship among older children; also glad of anything to further fill her time. To be alone and idle was to think and suffer.

Mrs. Pettigrew came in with Dr. Bellair one afternoon to watch the exercises.

"I don't see but what Vivian does the tricks as well as any of them," said her grandmother.

"She does beautifully," the doctor answered. "And her influence with the children is just what they needed. You see there's no romping and foolishness, and she sets the pace—starts them off when they're shy. I'm extremely obliged to her."

Mrs. Pettigrew watched Vivian's rhythmic movements, her erect carriage and swinging step, her warm color and sparkling eyes, as she led the line of happy youngsters and then turned upon the doctor.

"Huh!" she said.

At Susie's wedding, her childhood's friend was so far forgiven as to be chief bridesmaid, but seeing the happiness before her opened again the gates of her own pain.

When it was all over, and the glad young things were safely despatched upon their ribboned way, when all the guests had gone, when Mrs. St. Cloud felt the need of air and with the ever-gallant Mr. Skee set forth in search of it, when Dr. Bellair had returned to her patients, and Miss Orella to her own parlor, and was there consoled by Mr. Dykeman for the loss of her niece, then Vivian went to her room—all hers now, looking strangely large and empty—and set down among the drifts of white tissue paper and scattered pins—alone.

She sank down on the bed, weary and sad at heart, for an hour of full surrender long refused; meaning for once to let her grief have its full way with her. But, just as on the night of her hurried engagement she had been unable to taste to the full the happiness expected, so now, surrender as she might, she could not feel the intensity of expected pain.

She was lonely, unquestionably. She faced a lonely life. Six long, heavy months had passed since she had made her decision.

"I am nearly twenty-seven now," she thought, resignedly. "I shall never marry," and she felt a little shiver of the horror of last year.

But, having got this far in melancholy contemplation, her mind refused to dwell upon it, but filled in spite of her with visions of merry little ones, prancing in wavering circles, and singing their more wavering songs. She was lonely and a single woman—but she had something to do; and far more power to do it, more interest, enthusiasm, and skill, than at the season's beginning.

She thought of Morton—of what little they had heard since his hurried departure. He had gone farther West; they had heard of him in San Francisco, they had heard of him, after some months, in the Klondike region, then they had heard no more. He did not write. It seemed hard to so deeply hurt his aunt for what was no fault of hers; but Morton had never considered her feelings very deeply, his bitter anger, his hopelessness, his desperate disappointment, blinding him to any pain but his own.

But her thoughts of him failed to rouse any keen distinctive sorrow. They rambled backward and forward, from the boy who had been such a trouble to his aunt, such a continuous disappointment and mortification; to the man whose wooing, looked back upon at this distance, seemed far less attractive to the memory than it had been at the time. Even his honest attempt at improvement gave her but a feeling of pity, and though pity is akin to love it is not always a near relation.

From her unresisting descent into wells of pain, which proved unexpectedly shallow, the girl arose presently and quietly set to work arranging the room in its new capacity as hers only.

From black and bitter agony to the gray tastelessness of her present life was not an exciting change, but Vivian had more power in quiet endurance than in immediate resistance, and set herself now in earnest to fulfill the tasks before her.

This was March. She was planning an extension of her classes, the employment of an assistant. Her work was appreciated, her school increased. Patiently and steadily she faced her task, and found a growing comfort in it. When summer came, Dr. Bellair again begged her to help out in the plan of a girls' camp she was developing.

This was new work for Vivian, but her season in Mrs. Johnson's gymnastic class had given her a fresh interest in her own body and the use of it. That stalwart instructress, a large-boned, calm-eyed Swedish woman, was to be the manager of the camp, and Vivian this time, with a small salary attached, was to act as assistant.

"It's a wonderful thing the way people take to these camps," said Dr. Bellair. "They are springing up everywhere. Magnificent for children and young people."

"It is a wonderful thing to me," observed Mrs. Pettigrew. "You go to a wild place that costs no rent; you run a summer hotel without any accommodations; you get a lot of parents to pay handsomely for letting their children be uncomfortable—and there you are."

"They are not uncomfortable!" protested her friend, a little ruffled. "They like it. And besides liking it, it's good for them. It's precisely the roughing it that does them good."

It did do them good; the group of young women and girls who went to the high-lying mountain lake where Dr. Bellair had bought a piece of wild, rough country for her own future use, and none of them profited by it more than Vivian.

She had been, from time to time, to decorous "shore places," where one could do nothing but swim and lie on the sand; or to the "mountains," those trim, green, modest, pretty-picture mountains, of which New England is so proud; but she had never before been in an untouched wilderness.

Often in the earliest dawn she would rise from the springy, odorous bed of balsam boughs and slip out alone for her morning swim. A run through the pines to a little rocky cape, with a small cave she knew, and to glide, naked, into that glass-smooth water, warmer than the sunless air, and swim out softly, silently, making hardly a ripple, turn on her back and lie there—alone with the sky—this brought peace to her heart. She felt so free from every tie to earth, so like a soul in space, floating there with the clean, dark water beneath her, and the clear, bright heaven above her; and when the pale glow in the east brightened to saffron, warmed to rose, burst into a level blaze of gold, the lake laughed in the light, and Vivian laughed, too, in pure joy of being alive and out in all that glittering beauty.

She tramped the hills with the girls; picked heaping pails of wild berries, learned to cook in primitive fashion, slept as she had never slept in her life, from dark to dawn, grew brown and hungry and cheerful.

After all, twenty-seven was not an old age.

She came back at the summer-end, and Dr. Bellair clapped her warmly on the shoulder, declaring, "I'm proud of you, Vivian! Simply proud of you!"

Her grandmother, after a judicious embrace, held her at arm's length and examined her critically.

"I don't see but what you've stood it first rate," she admitted. "And if you *like* that color—why, you certainly are looking well."

She was well, and began her second year of teaching with a serene spirit.

In all this time of slow rebuilding Vivian would not have been left comfortless if masculine admiration could have pleased her. The young men at The Cottonwoods, now undistracted by Susie's gay presence, concentrated much devotion upon Vivian, as did also the youths across the way. She turned from them all, gently, but with absolute decision.

Among her most faithful devotees was young Percy Watson, who loved her almost as much as he loved Dr. Hale, and could never understand, in his guileless, boyish heart, why neither of them would talk about the other.

They did not forbid his talking, however, and the earnest youth, sitting in the quiet parlor at The Cottonwoods, would free his heart to Vivian about how the doctor worked too hard—sat up all hours to study—didn't give himself any rest—nor any fun.

"He'll break down some time—I tell him so. It's not natural for any man to work that way, and I don't see any real need of it. He says he's working on a book—some big medical book, I suppose; but what's the hurry? I wish you'd have him over here oftener, and make him amuse himself a little, Miss Vivian."

"Dr. Hale is quite welcome to come at any time—he knows that," said she.

Again the candid Percy, sitting on the doctor's shadowy piazza, poured out his devoted admiration for her to his silent host.

"She's the finest woman I ever knew!" the boy would say. "She's so beautiful and so clever, and so pleasant to everybody. She's *square*—like a man. And she's kind—like a woman, only kinder; a sort of motherliness about her. I don't see how she ever lived so long without being married. I'd marry her in a minute if I was good enough—and if she'd have me."

Dr. Hale tousled the ears of Balzac, the big, brown dog whose head was so often on his knee, and said nothing. He had not seen the girl since that night by the arbor.

Later in the season he learned, perforce, to know her better, and to admire her more.

Susie's baby came with the new year, and brought danger and anxiety. They hardly hoped to save the life of the child. The little mother was long unable to leave her bed. Since her aunt was not there, but gone, as Mrs. Dykeman, on an extended tour—"part business and part honeymoon," her husband told her—and since Mrs. Pettigrew now ruled alone at The Cottonwoods, with every evidence of ability and enjoyment, Vivian promptly installed herself in the Saunders home, as general housekeeper and nurse.

She was glad then of her strength, and used it royally, comforting the wretched Jim, keeping up Susie's spirits, and mothering the frail tiny baby with exquisite devotion.

Day after day the doctor saw her, sweet and strong and patient, leaving her school to the assistant, regardless of losses, showing the virtues he admired most in women.

He made his calls as short as possible; but even so, Vivian could not but note how his sternness gave way to brusque good cheer for the sick mother, and to a lovely gentleness with the child.

When that siege was over and the girl returned to her own work, she carried pleasant pictures in her mind, and began to wonder, as had so many others, why this man, who seemed so fitted to enjoy a family, had none.

She missed his daily call, and wondered further why he avoided them more assiduously than at first.

12

ACHIEVEMENTS

There are some folk born to beauty,
  And some to plenteous gold,
Some who are proud of being young,
  Some proud of being old.

Some who are glad of happy love,
  Enduring, deep and true,
And some who thoroughly enjoy
  The little things they do.

Upon all this Grandma Pettigrew cast an observant eye, and meditated sagely thereupon. Coming to a decision, she first took a course of reading in some of Dr. Bellair's big books, and then developed a series of perplexing symptoms, not of a too poignant or perilous nature, that took her to Dr. Hale's office frequently.

"You haven't repudiated Dr. Bellair, have you?" he asked her.

"I have never consulted Jane Bellair as a physician," she replied, "though I esteem her much as a friend."

The old lady's company was always welcome to him; he liked her penetrating eye, her close-lipped, sharp remarks, and appreciated the real kindness of her heart.

If he had known how closely she was peering into the locked recesses of his own, and how much she saw there, he would perhaps have avoided her as he did Vivian, and if he had known further that this ingenious old lady, pursuing long genealogical discussions with him, had finally unearthed a mutual old-time friend, and had forthwith started a correspondence with that friend, based on this common acquaintance in Carston, he might have left that city.

The old-time friend, baited by Mrs. Pettigrew's innocent comment on Dr. Hale's persistence in single blessedness, poured forth what she knew of the cause with no more embellishment than time is sure to give.

"I know why he won't marry," wrote she. "He had reason good to begin with, but I never dreamed he'd be obstinate enough to keep it up sixteen years. When he was a boy in college here I knew him well—he was a splendid fellow, one of the very finest. But he fell desperately in love with that beautiful Mrs. James—don't you remember about her? She married a St. Cloud later, and he left her, I think. She was as lovely as a cameo—and as hard and flat. That woman was the saintliest thing that ever breathed. She wouldn't live with her husband because he had done something wrong; she wouldn't get a divorce, nor let him, because that was wicked—and she always had a string of boys round her, and talked about the moral influence she had on them.

"Young Hale worshipped her—simply worshipped her—and she let him. She let them all. She had that much that was godlike about her—she loved incense. You need not ask for particulars. She was far too 'particular' for that. But one light-headed chap went and drowned himself—that was all hushed up, of course, but some of us felt pretty sure why. He was a half-brother to Dick Hale, and Dick was awfully fond of him. Then he turned hard and hateful all at once—used to talk horrid about women. He kept straight enough—that's easy for a misogynist, and studying medicine didn't help him any—doctors and ministers know too much about women. So there you are. But I'm astonished to hear he's never gotten over it; he always was obstinate—it's his only fault. They say he swore never to marry—if he did, that accounts. Do give my regards if you see him again."

Mrs. Pettigrew considered long and deeply over this information, as she slowly produced a jersey striped with Roman vividness. It was noticeable in this new life in Carston that Mrs. Pettigrew's knitted jackets had grown steadily brighter in hue from month to month.

Whereas, in Bainville, purple and brown were the high lights, and black, slate and navy blue the main colors; now her worsteds were as a painter's palette, and the result not only cheered, but bade fair to inebriate.

"A pig-headed man," she said to herself, as her needle prodded steadily in and out; "a pig-headed man, with a pig-headedness of sixteen years' standing. His hair must 'a turned gray from the strain of it. And there's Vivian, biddin' fair to be an old maid after all. What on *earth!*" She appeared to have forgotten that marriages are made in heaven, or to disregard that saying. "The Lord helps those that help themselves," was one of her favorite mottoes. "And much more those that help other people!" she used to add.

Flitting in and out of Dr. Hale's at all hours, she noted that he had a fondness for music, with a phenomenal incapacity to produce any. He encouraged his boys to play on any and every instrument the town afforded, and to sing, whether they could or not; and seemed never to weary of their attempts, though far from satisfied with the product.

"Huh!" said Mrs. Pettigrew.

Vivian could play, "Well enough to know better," she said, and seldom touched the piano. She had a deep, full, contralto voice, and a fair degree of training. But she would never make music unless she felt like it—and in this busy life, with so many people about her, she had always refused.

Grandma meditated.

She selected an evening when most of the boarders were out at some entertainment, and selfishly begged Vivian to stay at home with her—said she was feeling badly and wanted company. Grandma so seldom wanted anything that Vivian readily acquiesced; in fact, she was quite worried about her, and asked Dr. Bellair if she thought anything was the matter.

"She has seemed more quiet lately," said that astute lady, "and I've noticed her going in to Dr. Hale's during office hours. But perhaps it's only to visit with him."

"Are you in any pain, Grandma?" asked the girl, affectionately. "You're not sick, are you?"

"O, no—I'm not sick," said the old lady, stoutly. "I'm just—well, I felt sort of lonesome to-night—perhaps I'm homesick."

As she had never shown the faintest sign of any feeling for their deserted home, except caustic criticism and unfavorable comparison, Vivian rather questioned this theory, but she began to think there was something in it when her grandmother, sitting by the window in the spring twilight, began to talk of how this time of year always made her think of her girlhood.

"Time for the March peepers at home. It's early here, and no peepers anywhere that I've heard. 'Bout this time we'd be going to evening meeting. Seems as if I could hear that little old organ—and the singing!"

"Hadn't I better shut that window," asked Vivian. "Won't you get cold?"

"No, indeed," said her grandmother, promptly. "I'm plenty warm—I've got this little shawl around me. And it's so soft and pleasant out."

It was soft and pleasant, a delicious May-like night in March, full of spring scents and hints of coming flowers. On the dark piazza across the way she could make out a still figure sitting alone, and the thump of Balzac's heel as he struggled with his intimate enemies told her who it was.

"Come Ye Disconsolate," she began to hum, most erroneously. "How does that go, Vivian? I was always fond of it, even if I can't sing any more'n a peacock."

Vivian hummed it and gave the words in a low voice.

"That's good!" said the old lady. "I declare, I'm kinder hungry for some of those old hymns. I wish you'd play me some of 'em, Vivian."

So Vivian, glad to please her, woke the yellow keys to softer music than they were accustomed to, and presently her rich, low voice, sure, easy, full of quiet feeling, flowed out on the soft night air.

Grandma was not long content with the hymns. "I want some of those old-fashioned songs—you used to know a lot of 'em. Can't you do that 'Kerry Dance' of Molloy's, and 'Twickenham Ferry'—and 'Lauriger Horatius?'"

Vivian gave her those, and many another, Scotch ballads, English songs and German Lieder—glad to please her grandmother so easily, and quite unconscious of a dark figure which had crossed the street and come silently to sit on the farthest corner of their piazza.

Grandma, meanwhile, watched him, and Vivian as well, and then, with the most unsuspected suddenness, took to her bed. Sciatica, she said. An intermittent pain that came upon her so suddenly she couldn't stand up. She felt much better lying down, and Dr. Hale must attend her unceasingly.

This unlooked for overthrow of the phenomenally active old lady was a great blow to Mr. Skee; he showed real concern and begged to be allowed to see her.

"Why not?" said Mrs. Pettigrew. "It's nothing catching."

She lay, high-pillowed, as stiff and well arranged as a Knight Templar on a tombstone, arrayed for the occasion in a most decorative little dressing sack and ribbony night-cap.

"Why, ma'am," said Mr. Skee, "it's highly becomin' to you to be sick. It leads me to hope it's nothin' serious."

She regarded him enigmatically. "Is Dr. Hale out there, or Vivian?" she inquired in a low voice.

"No, ma'am—they ain't," he replied, after a glance in the next room.

Then he bent a penetrating eye upon her. She met it unflinchingly, but as his smile appeared and grew, its limitless widening spread contagion, and her calm front was broken.

"Elmer Skee," said she, with sudden fury, "you hold your tongue!"

"Ma'am!" he replied, "I have said nothin'—and I don't intend to. But if the throne of Europe was occupied by you, Mrs. Pettigrew, we would have a better managed world."

He proved a most agreeable and steady visitor during this period of confinement, and gave her full accounts of all that went on outside, with occasional irrelevant bursts of merriment which no rebuke from Mrs. Pettigrew seemed wholly to check.

He regaled her with accounts of his continuous consultations with Mrs. St. Cloud, and the wisdom and good taste with which she invariably advised him.

"Don't you admire a Platonic Friendship, Mrs. Pettigrew?"

"I do not!" said the old lady, sharply. "And what's more I don't believe you do."

"Well, ma'am," he answered, swaying backward and forward on the hind legs of his chair, "there are moments when I confess it looks improbable."

Mrs. Pettigrew cocked her head on one side and turned a gimlet eye upon him. "Look here, Elmer Skee," she said suddenly, "how much money have you really got?"

He brought down his chair on four legs and regarded her for a few moments, his smile widening slowly. "Well, ma'am, if I live through the necessary expenses involved on my present undertaking, I shall have about two thousand a year—if rents are steady."

"Which I judge you do not wish to be known?"

"If there's one thing more than another I have always admired in you, ma'am, it is the excellence of your judgment. In it I have absolute confidence."

Mrs. St. Cloud had some time since summoned Dr. Hale to her side for a severe headache, but he had merely sent word that his time was fully occupied, and recommended Dr. Bellair.

Now, observing Mrs. Pettigrew's tactics, the fair invalid resolved to take the bull by the horns and go herself to his office. She found him easily enough. He lifted his eyes as she entered, rose and stood with folded arms regarding her silently. The tall, heavy figure, the full beard, the glasses, confused even her excellent memory. After all it was many years since they had met, and he had been but one of a multitude.

She was all sweetness and gentle apology for forcing herself upon him, but really she had a little prejudice against women doctors—his reputation was so great—he was so temptingly near—she was in such pain—she had such perfect confidence in him—

He sat down quietly and listened, watching her from under his bent brows. Her eyes were dropped, her voice very weak and appealing; her words most perfectly chosen.

"I have told you," he said at length, "that I never treat women for their petty ailments, if I can avoid it."

She shook her head in grieved acceptance, and lifted large eyes for one of those penetrating sympathetic glances so frequently successful.

"How you must have suffered!" she said.

"I have," he replied grimly. "I have suffered a long time from having my eyes opened too suddenly to the brainless cruelty of women, Mrs. James."

She looked at him again, searchingly, and gave a little cry. "Dick Hale!" she said.

"Yes, Dick Hale. Brother to poor little Joe Medway, whose foolish young heart you broke, among others; whose death you are responsible for."

She was looking at him with widening wet eyes. "Ah! If you only knew how I, too, have suffered over that!" she said. "I was scarce more than a girl myself, then. I was careless, not heartless. No one knew what pain I was bearing, then. I liked the admiration of those nice boys—I never realized any of them would take it seriously. That has been a heavy shadow on my life, Dr. Hale—the fear that I was the thoughtless cause of that terrible thing. And you have never forgiven me. I do not wonder."

He was looking at her in grim silence again, wishing he had not spoken.

"So that is why you have never been to The Cottonwoods since I came," she pursued. "And I am responsible for all your loneliness. O, how dreadful!"

Again he rose to his feet.

"No, madam, you mistake. You were responsible for my brother's death, and for a bitter awakening on my part, but you are in no way responsible for my attitude since. That is wholly due to myself. Allow me again to recommend Dr. Jane Bellair, an excellent physician and even more accessible."

He held the door for her, and she went out, not wholly dissatisfied with her visit. She would have been far more displeased could she have followed his thoughts afterward.

"What a Consummate Ass I have been all my life!" he was meditating. "Because I met this particular type of sex parasite, to deliberately go sour—and forego all chance of happiness. Like a silly girl. A fool girl who says, 'I will never marry!' just because of some quarrel. But the girl never keeps her word. A man must."

The days were long to Vivian now, and dragged a little, for all her industry.

Mrs. St. Cloud tried to revive their former intimacy, but the girl could not renew it on the same basis. She, too, had sympathized with Mr. Dykeman, and now sympathized somewhat with Mr. Skee. But since that worthy man still volubly discoursed on Platonism, and his fair friend openly agreed in this view, there seemed no real ground for distress.

Mrs. Pettigrew remained ailing and rather captious. She had a telephone put at her bedside, and ran her household affairs efficiently, with Vivian as lieutenant, and the ever-faithful Jeanne to uphold the honor of the cuisine. Also she could consult her physician, and demanded his presence at all hours.

He openly ignored Mrs. St. Cloud now, who met his rude treatment with secret, uncomplaining patience.

Vivian spoke of this. "I do not see why he need be so rude, Grandma. He may hate women, but I don't see why he should treat her so shamefully."

"Well, I do," replied the invalid, "and what's more I'm going to show you; I've always disliked that woman, and now I know why. I'd turn her out of the house if it wasn't for Elmer Skee. That man's as good as gold under all his foolishness, and if he can get any satisfaction out of that meringue he's welcome. Dr. Hale doesn't hate women, child, but a woman broke his heart once—and then he made an idiot of himself by vowing never to marry."

She showed her friend's letter, and Vivian read it with rising color. "O, Grandma! Why that's worse than I ever thought—even after what Dr. Bellair told us. And it was his brother! No wonder he's so fond of boys. He tries to warn them, I suppose."

"Yes, and the worst of it is that he's really got over his grouch; and he's in love—but tied down by that foolish oath, poor man."

"Is he, Grandma? How do you know? With whom?"

"You dear, blind child!" said the old lady, "with you, of course. Has been ever since we came."

The girl sat silent, a strange feeling of joy rising in her heart, as she reviewed the events of the last two years. So that was why he would not stay that night. And that was why. "No wonder he wouldn't come here!" she said at length. "It's on account of that woman. But why did he change?"

"Because she went over there to see him. He wouldn't come to her. I heard her 'phone to him one evening." The old lady chuckled. "So she marched herself over there—I saw her, and I guess she got her needin's. She didn't stay long. And his light burned till morning."

"Do you think he cares for her, still?"

"Cares for her!" The old lady fairly snorted her derision. "He can't bear the sight of her—treats her as if she wasn't there. No, indeed. If he did she'd have him fast enough, now. Well! I suppose he'll repent of that foolishness of his all the days of his life—and stick it out! Poor man."

Mrs. Pettigrew sighed, and Vivian echoed the sigh. She began to observe Dr. Hale with new eyes; to study little matters of tone and manner—and could not deny her grandmother's statement. Nor would she admit it—yet.

The old lady seemed weaker and more irritable, but positively forbade any word of this being sent to her family.

"There's nothing on earth ails me," she said. "Dr. Hale says there's not a thing the matter that he can see—that if I'd only eat more I'd get stronger. I'll be all right soon, my dear. I'll get my appetite and get well, I have faith to believe."

She insisted on his coming over in the evening, when not too busy, and staying till she dropped asleep, and he seemed strangely willing to humor her; sitting for hours in the quiet parlor, while Vivian played softly, and sang her low-toned hymns.

So sitting, one still evening, when for some time no fretful "not so loud" had come from the next room, he turned suddenly to Vivian and asked, almost roughly—"Do you hold a promise binding?—an oath, a vow—to oneself?"

She met his eyes, saw the deep pain there, the long combat, the irrepressible hope and longing.

"Did you swear to keep your oath secret?" she asked.

"Why, no," he said, "I did not. I will tell you. I did not swear never to tell a woman I loved her. I never dreamed I should love again. Vivian, I was fool enough to love a shallow, cruel woman, once, and nearly broke my heart in consequence. That was long years ago. I have never cared for a woman since—till I met you. And now I must pay double for that boy folly."

He came to her and took her hand.

"I love you," he said, his tense grip hurting her. "I shall love you as long as I live—day and night—forever! You shall know that at any rate!"

She could not raise her eyes. A rich bright color rose to the soft border of her hair. He caught her face in his hands and made her look at him; saw those dark, brilliant eyes softened, tear-filled, asking, and turned sharply away with a muffled cry.

"I have taken a solemn oath," he said in a strained, hard voice, "never to ask a woman to marry me."

He heard a little gasping laugh, and turned upon her. She stood there smiling, her hands reached out to him.

"You don't have to," she said.

A LONG TIME later, upon their happy stillness broke a faint voice from the other room:

"Vivian, I think if you'd bring me some bread and butter—and a cup of tea—and some cold beef and a piece of pie—I could eat it."

UPON THE RAPID and complete recovery of her grandmother's health, and the announcement of Vivian's engagement, Mr. and Mrs. Lane decided to make a visit to their distant mother and daughter, hoping as well that Mr. Lane's cough might be better for a visit in that altitude. Mr. and Mrs. Dykeman also sent word of their immediate return.

Jeanne, using subtle powers of suggestion, caused Mrs. Pettigrew to decide upon giving a dinner, in honor of these events. There was the betrothed couple, there were the honored guests; there were Jimmie and Susie, with or without the baby; there were the Dykemans; there was Dr. Bellair, of course; there was Mr. Skee, an even number.

"I'm sorry to spoil that table, but I've got to take in Mrs. St. Cloud," said the old lady.

"O, Grandma! Why! It'll spoil it for Dick."

"Huh!" said her grandmother. "He's so happy you couldn't spoil it with a mummy. If I don't ask her it'll spoil it for Mr. Skee."

So Mrs. St. Cloud made an eleventh at the feast, and neither Mr. Dykeman nor Vivian could find it in their happy hearts to care.

Mr. Skee arose, looking unusually tall and shapely in immaculate every-day dress, his well-brushed hair curling vigorously around the little bald spots; his smile wide and benevolent.

"Ladies and Gentlemen, both Domestic and Foreign, Friends and Fellowtownsmen and Women—Ladies, God Bless 'em; also Children, if any: I feel friendly enough tonight to include the beasts of the fields—but such would be inappropriate at this convivial board—among these convivial boarders.

"This is an occasion of great rejoicing. We have many things to rejoice over, both great *and* small. We have our healths; all of us, apparently. We are experiencing the joys of reunion—in the matter of visiting parents that is, and long absent daughters.

"We have also the Return of the Native, in the shape of my old friend Andy—now become a Benedict—and seeming to enjoy it. About this same Andy I have a piece of news to give you which will cause you astonishment and gratification, but which involves me in a profuse apology—a most sincere and general apology.

"You know how a year or more ago it was put about in this town that Andrew Dykeman was a ruined man?" Mrs. St. Cloud darted a swift glance at Mr. Dykeman, but his eyes rested calmly on his wife; then at Mr. Skee—but he was pursuing his remorseful way.

"I do not wish to blame my friend Andy for his reticence—but he certainly did exhibit reticence on this occasion—to beat the band! *He* never contradicted this rumor—not once. He just went about looking kind o' down in the mouth for some reason or other, and when for the sake o' Auld Lang Syne I offered him a job in my office—the cuss took it! I won't call this deceitful, but it sure was reticent to a degree.

"Well Ladies—and Gentlemen—the best of us are liable to mistakes, and I have to admit—I am glad to humble myself and make this public admission—I was entirely in error in this matter.

"It wasn't so. There was nothing in it. It was rumor, pure and simple. Andy Dykeman never lost no mine, it appears; or else he had another up his sleeve concealed from his best friends. Anyhow, the facts are these; not only that A. Dykeman as he sits before you is a prosperous and wealthy citizen, but that he has been, for these ten years back, and we were all misled by a mixture of rumor and reticence. If he has concealed these facts from the wife of his bosom I submit that that is carrying reticence too far!" Again Mrs. St. Cloud sent a swift glance at the reticent one, and again caught only his tender apologetic look toward his wife, and her utter amazement.

Mr. Dykeman rose to his feet.

"I make no apologies for interrupting my friend," he said. "It is necessary at times. He at least can never be accused of reticence. Neither do I make apologies for letting rumor take its course—a course often interesting to observe. But I do apologize—in this heartfelt and public manner, to my wife, for marrying her under false pretenses. But any of you gentlemen who have ever had any experience in the attitude of," he hesitated mercifully, and said, "the World, toward a man with money, may understand what it meant to me, after many years of bachelorhood, to find a heart that not only loved me for myself alone, but absolutely loved me better because I'd lost my money—or she thought I had. I have hated to break the charm. But now my unreticent friend here has stated the facts, and I make my confession. Will you forgive me, Orella?"

"Speech! Speech!" cried Mr. Skee. But Mrs. Dykeman could not be persuaded to do anything but blush and smile and squeeze her husband's hand under the table, and Mr. Skee arose once more.

"This revelation being accomplished," he continued cheerfully; "and no one any the worse for it, as I see," he was not looking in the direction of Mrs. St. Cloud, whose slippered foot beat softly under the table, though her face wore its usual sweet expression, possibly a trifle strained; "I now proceed to a proclamation of that happy event to celebrate which we are here gathered together. I allude to the Betrothal of Our Esteemed Friend, Dr. Richard Hale, and the Fairest of the Fair! Regarding the Fair, we think he has chosen well. But regarding Dick Hale, his good fortune is so clear, so evidently undeserved, and his pride and enjoyment thereof so ostentatious, as to leave us some leeway to make remarks.

"Natural remarks, irresistible remarks, as you might say, and not intended to be acrimonious. Namely, such as these: It's a long lane that has no turning; There's many a slip 'twixt the cup and the lip; The worm will turn; The pitcher that goes too often to the well gets broken at last; Better Late than Never. And so on and so forth. Any other gentleman like to make remarks on this topic?"

Dr. Hale rose, towering to his feet.

"I think I'd better make them," he said. "No one else could so fully, so heartily, with such perfect knowledge point out how many kinds of a fool I've been for all these years. And yet of them all there are only two that I regret—this last two in which if I had been wiser, perhaps I might have found my happiness sooner. As that cannot be proven, however, I will content myself with the general acknowledgment that Bachelors are Misguided Bats, I myself having long been the worst instance; women, in general, are to be loved and honored; and that I am proud and glad to accept your congratulations because the sweetest and noblest woman in the world has honored me with her love."

"I never dreamed you could put so many words together, Doc—and really make sense!" said Mr. Skee, genially, as he rose once more. "You certainly show a proper spirit at last, and all is forgiven. But now, my friends; now if your attention is not exhausted, I have yet another Event to confide to you.

Mr. and Mrs. Lane wore an aspect of polite interest. Susie and Jim looked at each other with a sad but resigned expression. So did Mrs. Dykeman and her husband. Vivian's hand was in her lover's and she could not look unhappy, but they, too, deprecated this last announcement, only too well anticipated. Only Mrs. St. Cloud, her fair face bowed in gentle confusion, showed anticipating pleasure.

Mr. Skee waved his hand toward her with a large and graceful gesture.

"You must all of you have noticed the amount of Platonic Friendship which has been going on for some time between my undeserving self and this lovely lady here. Among so many lovely ladies perhaps I'd better specify that I refer to the one on my left.

"What she has been to me, in my lonely old age, none of you perhaps realize." He wore an expression as of one long exiled, knowing no one who could speak his language.

"She has been my guide, counsellor and friend; she has assisted me with advice most wise and judicious; she has not interfered with my habits, but has allowed me to enjoy life in my own way, with the added attraction of her companionship.

"Now, I dare say, there may have been some of you who have questioned my assertion that this friendship was purely Platonic. Perhaps even the lady herself, knowing the heart of man, may have doubted if my feeling toward her was really friendship."

Mr. Skee turned his head a little to one side and regarded her with a tender inquiring smile.

To this she responded sweetly: "Why no, Mr. Skee, of course, I believed what you said."

"There, now," said he, admiringly. "What is so noble as the soul of woman? It is to this noble soul in particular, and to all my friends here in general, that I now confide the crowning glory of a long and checkered career, namely, and to wit, that I am engaged to be married to that

Peerless Lady, Mrs. Servilla Pettigrew, of whose remarkable capacities and achievements I can never sufficiently express my admiration."

A silence fell upon the table. Mr. Skee sat down smiling, evidently in cheerful expectation of congratulations. Mrs. Pettigrew wore an alert expression, as of a skilled fencer preparing to turn any offered thrusts. Mrs. St. Cloud seemed to be struggling with some emotion, which shook her usual sweet serenity. The others, too, were visibly affected, and not quick to respond.

Then did Mr. Saunders arise with real good nature and ever-ready wit; and pour forth good-humored nonsense with congratulations all around, till a pleasant atmosphere was established, in which Mrs. St. Cloud could so far recover as to say many proper and pretty things; sadly adding that she regretted her imminent return to the East would end so many pleasant friendships.

ABOUT THE AUTHOR

Widely considered a period of florescence for feminist writing in the United States, the late nineteenth century and the early twentieth saw the appearance of works by such authors as Kate Chopin, Sarah Orne Jewett, Willa Cather, Gertrude Stein, and Charlotte Perkins Gilman. As a lecturer, writer, activist and poet, Gilman played a major part in articulating the role of women in an era of great upheaval, including rapid industrialization, urbanization, and a changing topography of private and public life. Best known for her short story "The Yellow Wallpaper" and her socialist-feminist treatise *Women and Economics*, Gilman was also the author of many other works of fiction and nonfiction that contributed to the shape and structure of American politics. The jagged edges and uneven terrain of her work, both in aesthetic and in political terms, is as interesting as its quantity.

ABOUT THE EDITOR

Dana Seitler is Assistant Professor of Literary Theory and Cultural Studies at Wayne State University.

Library of Congress Cataloging-in-Publication Data

Gilman, Charlotte Perkins, 1860–1935.

The crux / Charlotte Perkins Gilman ; introduction by Dana Seitler.

p. cm.

ISBN 0-8223-3179-9 (cloth : alk. paper)

ISBN 0-8223-3167-5 (pbk. : alk. paper)

1. Boardinghouses—Fiction. 2. Sexually transmitted diseases—Fiction. 3. Women pioneers—Fiction. 4. Massachusetts—Fiction. 5. Colorado—Fiction. 6. Sex role—Fiction. 7. Eugenics—Fiction. I. Title.

PS1744.G57C78 2003   813′.4—dc21   2002155864